A LOVE SO TRUE

Marooned in a lonely Dales farm-house, in blizzard conditions, on a fell-walking challenge is not Tania Selwood's idea of a perfect holiday — especially as her co-leader Jake Anderson clearly resents her input into the welfare of their young charges. She struggles to hide her growing feelings for him as she fights to convince him they should stay. Can the beauty of their surroundings work its magic on them and make them realise their future happiness lies with each other?

*Books by Sheila Spencer-Smith
in the Linford Romance Library:*

THE PEBBLE BANK

SHEILA SPENCER-SMITH

A LOVE SO TRUE

Complete and Unabridged

LINFORD
Leicester

First published in Great Britain in 2011

First Linford Edition
published 2013

British Library CIP Data

Spencer-Smith, Sheila.
    A love so true.- -(Linford romance library)
    1. Love stories.
    2. Large type books.
    I. Title II. Series
    823.9'2–dc23

    ISBN 978–1–4448–1434–7

Published by
F. A. Thorpe (Publishing)
Anstey, Leicestershire

Set by Words & Graphics Ltd.
Anstey, Leicestershire
Printed and bound in Great Britain by
T. J. International Ltd., Padstow, Cornwall

Gentle Persuasion

Tania glanced up at the glistening snow on Rigg Bank where, with joyful abandon, bodies hurled themselves down as if there were no tomorrow. Her young brother's scarlet toboggan felt as if it was raring to go too, she thought, just like Max. She smiled to see him acting his age for the first time in weeks. This was exactly what he needed to help in the healing process.

'Come on, Tania, we're wasting good time just looking,' Max cried, his cheeks glowing in the icy air. 'What are we waiting for?'

The snow scrunched beneath their feet as Tania unlatched the gate in the wall and they began to climb the hill. Halfway up she stopped, breathless. 'This'll do for a start, Max,' she said.

He let out a startled squeak as he set off, gradually gaining speed and landing in the soft snow at the bottom. Watching him trudge back up again, she remembered how she had felt when she was nine years old.

That first panicky moment and then the joy of sky and earth merging as if she were flying out of this world with no thought of anything but the present moment. Wonderful!

She laughed as he reached her once more, keen to have another go. Her spirits rose sky-high too as she watched her brother zoom off again, glad that he was happy for a few moments at least. If only this white hillside could stay like this forever.

She gazed down at the village in the distance, pleased that for this weekend at least she had been able to come tobogganing on Rigg Bank just as she had every winter when she was growing up.

'Watch it, Gregor!' a voice boomed out as a wooden sled hissed past her far too close.

She leapt to one side and stood holding her arms tightly against her for warmth as she watched Max climb back up to her once more. After that they moved further up the hillside to get longer runs.

'My turn now,' she cried after a while, pushing her loose hair behind her ears as she sat down on the toboggan and prepared for the sheer joy of speed.

Down she went, the colours of the other participants' clothes merging in streaks at the side of her eyes as the bottom of the hill came racing up fast to meet her.

Suddenly there was a crack like thunder and she was in a welter of flaying arms and legs as she slithered away from the toboggan into a heap of snow at one side. She lay there, bemused and gasping. The shouting tore the cold air around her into a thousand pieces.

Max's voice seemed to be coming from a long way away. 'Tania, are you all right?'

'Can I help?' asked a strange voice from above.

She was conscious of the dark hair in

fashionable peaks and the disconcertingly blue eyes of the man looking down at her. For a moment he looked concerned, but then he seemed to think better of it and to weigh several things in the balance.

'I'm fine, really,' she said as she struggled for breath. What an idiot! She tried to sit up at up but her arms felt too weak to push against the snow.

'Here, let me,' he said.

'No, no, really I'm all right . . . '

'I don't think so.' He grabbed her arms and pulled her to a standing position, holding her against him for a moment. She felt colour flood her cheeks as she tried to pull free.

'Wait, can't you? You'll be fine in a minute.'

Tania rubbed her hands across her eyes and wished the white hillside would keep still. Max stirred the remains of his toboggan with his toe, trying not to cry. Slowly the mist cleared and she took a deep breath.

He let go of her. 'OK now?'

She nodded. The penetrating way he looked at her was disturbing so that her need to prove she could cope was suddenly important.

'That boy on the sled's a menace,' she said. 'Is he with you? He's smashed my brother's toboggan.'

He frowned. 'You should have controlled it better, leant to one side to keep clear.'

'I had no chance to get out of his way.'

'If you say so.'

At least he could have apologised on behalf of his son, she thought. Instead he blamed her for the mishap, standing there in the snow like an arrogant giant.

'Give me your address and I'll see you're reimbursed,' he said.

She raised her chin defiantly. 'No way.' She wasn't accepting compensation from anyone who accused her of incompetence. She'd rather buy Max a hundred new toboggans.

The others who had gathered round began to move away now and the hillside rang with activity again. She felt the ground shiver and turn grey. She turned her back, not trusting herself to say more.

The day was no longer glorious. Even the snow had dimmed and dark clouds covered the sky. She pulled at the rope of the toboggan and it shot towards her, a crushed red thing.

'Come on, Max,' she said. 'We're going home.'

To Tania's astonishment her friend's Corsa was parked outside their house. With her boots off but still in her bulky jacket, she went into the kitchen to discover what Annie was doing here when she'd be seeing her in town next day.

Her father looked up and smiled as the door opened. Then he glanced at the dark-haired young woman in glasses seated opposite.

On the table between them was a Black Forest gateau, a quarter of it gone, oozing cream. With one hand Annie plucked a red cherry off its chocolate background, and popped it in her mouth. 'Naughty,' she said. 'Hello Max.'

'Did *you* bring the cake?' asked Max, wide-eyed.

She laughed comfortably. 'Lucky you came back now while there's still some left. Can I come with you next time?'

'It's no use,' he said. 'My toboggan's a write-off.'

Annie was at once sympathetic. 'Oh poor Max! Have a piece of cake.' She cut him a generous slice, slipped it on a plate and pushed it across to him.

Tania filled in the details about the incident, shrugging herself out of her jacket at the same time and sitting down. 'It was too bad blaming me for it,' she said. 'I think that boy on the sled crashed into me on purpose.'

Max, eating cake, seemed unworried, but her father looked at Tania in concern. 'An accident surely?'

She didn't want to push it even though she still felt shaken at the experience. The man had been concerned for her at first, she was sure of it. Then he had seemed to condone the boy's callous behaviour and to assume that she could have prevented the outcome if she had had more sense.

'I suppose so,' she said and smiled at him to show she held no hard feelings so that the anxious frown vanished from his forehead. Dad had enough worries at the moment and she wasn't going to add to them. What was the price of a new toboggan compared with that?

She leaned forward. 'So Annie, are you going to tell us why you're here when I'm coming back tomorrow?'

To help her father and young brother after her mother's death, Tania had moved back temporarily to the family home, but now she was due to return to her life in Oxingley and the flat she had shared with Annie, a nurse at the local hospital, for the past two years.

Fortunately the daily commute from here to her secretarial work at the comprehensive school twenty miles away had been manageable. Was her timing to return the right thing to do as Dad insisted? She still felt anxious about how Max would cope.

Annie took off her glasses and gave them a quick wipe on the sleeve of her thick jersey. 'You know my cousin, Jake?'

'Jake the Achiever?'

'Jake can't help being ambitious,' said Annie defensively.

'I know, Annie. Sorry. I'm sure he's a great guy.'

'He's doing really well with that architects' firm in Leeds. You'd like him. He's into helping disadvantaged kids in his spare time. They're taking part in a fell walk for a few days up in the Dales at half term, setting off next Saturday.'

'That's the week you're on your course in York.'

'Exactly. That's why I can't go with them. Just think how useful I'd be if anyone fell off a precipice or suc-cumbed to pneumonia or something.

I'd have volunteered like a shot.'

Tania laughed. 'Don't give me that. You loathe walking. I know you too well.'

'But *you* love it, Tania, and you like children,' Annie said, ignoring the jibe. 'I suppose you wouldn't be working in a school if you hated them.'

Tania looked at her, a dreadful suspicion dawning. 'You don't mean . . . '

Annie pushed her glasses back to the bridge of her nose as if this would give her courage. 'Jake needs your help.'

'He needs *my* help?'

'The other leader's had to pull out because of her injured foot.'

'And?'

'They can't take part if Jake can't find a replacement quickly.'

'You want me to take her place?' Tania said in indignation. 'You really are the limit, Annie.'

Annie shifted a little in her seat. 'Oh please say you will, Tania. It's really important.'

'It's too much to ask,' said Tania. 'I'll

be here looking after Max at half term. Tell her, Dad.'

'I don't see why you can't take part if we can make other arrangements,' he said. 'It's an opportunity.'

'For what?' She looked at him in dismay and saw the sadness in his eyes. This was a golden chance for doing something helpful, as Mum would have said. As Dad was now saying in her place because she was no longer here.

'And you can take Max with you, Tania,' said Annie triumphantly.

'I can go too?' cried Max. 'Oh *great*.'

Tania looked from one to the other and then back at her brother's eager face. She got up and lifted the lid of the slow cooker on the worktop to give her time to think.

A rush of lamb-scented steam made her eyes water. Dad had been up early getting this going and it smelt delicious. She replaced the lid and stood leaning against the unit.

'You're ganging up on me,' she said.

11

'Think about it,' her father said, standing up too. 'I can manage fine for a few days without the pair of you.'

She looked at his careworn face. 'You really want us to take part, Dad?'

His face lit up as he smiled. 'Why not, lass? It'll be good for Max and you, too, I shouldn't wonder.'

Tania gazed at him in silence. Dad was so unselfish it wasn't true.

'Lunch in half an hour,' he said. 'You'll join us, Annie? We'll leave them to it until then, lad, to talk things through. Come on.'

Reluctantly Max went with him.

* * *

'Think what an adventure it'll be for Max,' Annie said when they had closed the door behind them and Tania sat down again. 'He'll have a great time. You'll be spending the nights in remote places in bunk houses, that sort of thing. He'll love it.'

'But he's only nine.'

Annie shrugged. 'The snow's beginning to thaw already so that won't be a
problem.'

'You're serious about this, aren't you?
How old are these kids?'

'About fourteen, I think.' Annie stuck
her finger in the gooey chocolate of
what remained of the gateau and licked
it. 'You can cope, Tania. Easy-peasy.'

'It's all right for you to say.'

'Those kids'll be so disappointed if
they can't go.'

'Emotional blackmail now, is it?'

Annie grinned. 'Would I stoop to
such a thing?'

'You ask me that?'

Annie leaned forward an earnest
expression on her face now. 'Please,
Tania. Think how hard it'll be to find
anyone else as suitable as you at such
short notice. You're so right because
you've got the required checks already
in place because of working in a
school.'

Tania gazed at her friend. 'Well yes, I
see. You have a point.'

'And you like fell walking. That sort of thing. You're the perfect answer. So can I say yes for the moment and you can make a final decision later?'

'If you insist.'

'Great! And you'll come back earlier tomorrow for the planning meeting at our place? Jake'll fill you in on all the details then.'

Tania smiled. 'I must be mad,' she said.

She couldn't help a little stir of excitement to equal her brother's as the afternoon wore on and she had the chance to think more deeply about what she had let herself in for.

She had only to look at Max assembling a pile of jerseys and scarves on his bed to know that it would take more courage than she possessed to pull out now. To deny him this opportunity would be cruel.

She would need to get them both kitted out with thick socks, waterproof trousers and sleeping bags. Bunkhouses were likely to be primitive places and the weather sure to be cold in those high, exposed areas.

She'd take her camera with her too. Photos of any spectacular views could make good subjects for her water-colours when she got back. The tutor at art class often suggested this. Her fellow-student, Ivan, was planning to use his camera in Florence to good effect and had told her so when they'd had coffee together after the art class as usual the last time she was there.

When they first met she had liked the way Ivan's mouth twitched when he thought of something amusing to say and she was glad when he had sought her company. After that it became their habit to make for the Blue Orchid Café after the class each Tuesday evening.

Soon they met at other times too. She liked his kind manner and the way he seemed to know that any emotional involvement was difficult for her at the present moment and made no attempt to rush things.

He had been sadly disappointed

when she had turned down his invitation to join the Florence trip during the half term break that the art class tutor was arranging.

Briefly, she had thought of the pleasure of being in a group of like-minded people, enjoying the beauty of a place she had long wanted to visit. And surely the sky would be blue and the air less icy than it was likely to be here the last week in February?

She had struggled to keep the disappointment out of her voice as she told him that she couldn't come because she'd promised to be at home for Max at half term and they needed to be in a familiar place at this difficult time.

He took her hand and gave it a squeeze. 'Of course. Poor Max.'

She had smiled, grateful for his understanding. So what would Ivan think now of her proposed trek over the Pennines?

'It's the Chance of a Lifetime'

'Jake's not coming,' said Annie on Sunday evening. She snapped the lid shut on her mobile phone, threw it on the sofa and slumped down beside it.

Tania looked up from searching the bottom of her bag for her special biro. 'Jake the Achiever? Is he too busy redesigning the Taj Mahal or sussing out the highest peak in Yorkshire for a new housing estate?'

'Not in the dark,' said Annie, giggling.

'What then?' Tania found her biro and looked round for her pad.

'Some excuse about a client he had to see urgently. How weak is that? You'd think he'd want to put you in the picture himself about this fell walking thing, wouldn't you?' Annie sounded thoroughly put out.

'He's probably afraid I'll abscond if

he tells me all the grisly details.' Tania found what she was looking for and sat down on the nearest chair.

Annie looked at her over her glasses, letting them slip down her nose before hitching them up again. 'You're not mad at me for landing you in it?'

'What's this, cold feet on my behalf? I'll have you know Dad's lent me some extra thick socks. So, Jake the Achiever isn't going to show up? How about you filling me in on some of the things you know about it instead, Annie, like the names of the rest of the team?'

'OK then,' said Annie, ticking them off on her fingers. 'Colette's had a run of bad luck when her father died and now she's living with an aunt whose health's none too good and she'll have to be re-housed or something gruesome. I don't know all the details, but it doesn't sound good. And her friend, Becky's fourteen too, and Wayne. And I think Gregor's fifteen.'

'Gregor?' said Tania, wrinkling her nose as she tried to remember where

18

she had heard that name recently.

A picture of a snowy hillside shot into her mind and she heard again the hiss of metal runners on snow. She gazed at her friend in horror. 'Oh no, I don't believe it.'

'What's wrong?' said Annie, alarmed.

'He sounds like the boy who crashed into me up on Rigg Bank,' said Tania in dismay. 'Gregor's not a common name. Were Gregor and his father sledging up on Rigg Bank yesterday too?'

Annie pushed up her glasses on the bridge of her nose again. 'Jake's not his father. He most likely took the boy and the others sledging as a favour. Jake does things like that.'

'So that was your cousin, Jake?' Tania leaned back and closed her eyes. Behind her eyelids she could see the man clearly looking down at her as she lay in the snow. He would have looked threatening if it hadn't been for his anxious expression.

A chill of horror ran down her spine at another disconcerting thought. He would have seen her flying down the hill on a child's plastic toboggan screaming with delight. Jake, the man who accused her unfairly of not being in control of her toboggan and whom she had all but accused of being a thug like his supposed son! No wonder he planned to be absent tonight. He was obviously leaving it to his cousin, Annie, to break the news that her presence on the fell walking exercise would not be welcome.

'That's me finished then,' she said, surprised at her disappointment. 'I made a right fool of myself on Rigg Bank. You might as well admit it, Annie.'

'Admit what?'

'That I'm no longer needed. I lost it yesterday when Gregor smashed into me. Jake won't want me after that.'

'Why not?' said Annie. 'Jake's nothing if not fair. And he's desperate.'

'Desperate? In what way desperate?'

'Not in the way you're thinking, I'll have you know,' said Annie with spirit.

'Strings of women hanging on his every word?'

'Who knows? He's handsome enough. And amusing when he gets going. You'll like him. He's always on the go doing interesting things.'

Tania frowned. 'So you think he's so keen to get this thing off the ground that he'll have me no matter what?' Her opinion of him began to drop even further.

What sort of person was willing to put his charges in the care of a stupid woman? But she was relieved that she wouldn't after all have to explain to Max exactly why they couldn't take part.

Annie leapt up. 'I'll get the kettle on and then fill you in on the things Jake told me to tell you.'

★　★　★

Tania was early arriving her art class on Tuesday, aware that she hadn't been able to attend for the past weeks and feeling at a distinct disadvantage. By the time Ivan arrived she had settled herself in the back row and had her painting table organised.

His face lit up when he saw her. 'Oh Tania, it's great to see you. I've missed you.'

She smiled and moved her chair a little to give him room to get to the table next to hers.

He said no more as he removed his box of paint tubes from his backpack and then lay each one out in front of him with care.

The subject this evening was veiling and because of what lay ahead of her next week, Tania watched the tutor give a demonstration of the technique without really taking much in. Ivan, however, was pleased with his painting of the sunset over the sea.

Tania viewed her own effort with dislike, wishing she had some of Ivan's patience. She hadn't bothered to queue for the hair dryer to facilitate the drying of her work and, adding the next layer too quickly, had ended up with a cauliflower effect she didn't want.

'Coffee?' Ivan said as they began to pack up.

Tania shook her head. 'Not tonight, Ivan.'

He looked disappointed. 'Just a quick one? I haven't seen you for so long. We've a lot of catching up to do.'

'Another time,' she said. 'I'm sorry, Ivan, but I've only just got back to Oxingley as you know, and there are things to do.'

'I've been thinking, Tania. You know there's a cancellation on our Florence trip? Couldn't your aunt in Leeds look after Max for the few days we'll be away?'

She shook her head. 'I can't ask her.'

'Why not?'

'Because she's done such a lot for us already. She deserves a rest.'

'I've been on to the Uffizi Gallery website and we can book tickets before we go to save queuing,' he said, his face shining with enthusiasm. 'They only let

23

in a certain number of people at a time so you don't need to worry about crowds.'

She looked at him, so well meaning, friendly, and anxious to please, and knew that she didn't want this. 'But I promised Dad faithfully to be there for Max,' she said. 'I'm sorry, Ivan,'

'It's the chance of a lifetime, Tania, don't you see?'

For a moment she was silent. It would be so easy to fall in with his plans. Aunty Janet would agree, she was sure, but Max would be on his own with her in that large Victorian mausoleum of a house and he'd hate that. She couldn't bear to think of him there fighting back his misery while she was off enjoying herself.

'Surely your father won't hold you back, once he knows about this last minute chance?'

She shook her head, feeling a flash of annoyance at his unfair assumption. Dad didn't even know there was a chance to go in the first place and she had no intention of discussing it with him now.

She sighed. 'It's not like that, Ivan. I'm off next week, too. I'm taking Max on a fell walking challenge up in the Dales.'

He looked at her in astonishment. 'So when was this arranged?'

'Only on Saturday. There's a lot to prepare.'

'And don't you think I have a lot to prepare, going all the way to Florence?'

'I'm really sorry, Ivan. I don't want us to go on like this anymore. We don't seem to be going anywhere . . . '

'Certainly not together,' he said with a bitterness that surprised her.

'I'm sorry,' she said again.

'Me too.' He hoisted his bag onto his shoulder and turned away.

She could tell from the hard line to his shoulders that Ivan would never really understand the loving responsibility she felt for her brother. He was a good man, but sometimes he was too sure of himself in thinking of what was best for others.

For a moment she stayed where she was, watching him go. Then, picking up her own painting gear, she left the building deep in thought.

The Journey Begins

Max, bright-eyed and excited, was early at the station yard from where they were due to set off in the Land Rover to the starting point of the walk higher up the dale. As Tania arrived their father who had brought him patted his son's shoulder in farewell.

'Take good care of him, lass,' he said to her.

Kitted out in her blue cagoule with her woolly hat perched on top of her hair, she smiled at him. 'Would I do anything else, Dad?' she said.

Dad looked serious for a moment. 'That's my girl.'

She hated seeing him leave, but he had to be at work at the Garden Centre at nine. The others were all arriving now anyway and a Land Rover was drawing up.

The door opened and a man who

could only be Jake jumped out. As he slammed shut the door she recognised him immediately in his dark green jacket, the same one he had been wearing on Rigg Bank.

His eyes met Tania's in a long speculative gaze. She stood up straight, determined not to look like the pathetic wimp he obviously thought she was.

'All set?' he said, his voice crisp.

He looked exceptionally fit with his boots freshly waxed and his grey hiking trousers tucked into thick brown socks.

'All set,' she repeated.

'And the lad?

'Raring to go.'

He nodded, making no mention of their last fraught meeting. 'I understand that Annie has filled you in on the details?'

'She has.' She studied him through half-closed eyes, trying to get his measure. Definitely sure of himself. His height and build would inspire confidence in others too, she was sure.

She couldn't imagine this man not

28

knowing his own mind and what was good for everyone else. He didn't like wasting words either.

'Come on then, you lot,' said Jake. 'What are you waiting for?' He began lifting some of the heavier bags into the vehicle. When only hers was left she handed it to him. He took it and his fingers, brushing hers, felt warm.

He paused for a moment as if he was about to say something significant. Then, changing his mind, hauled it inside with the others.

Gregor scowled at the ground. 'I want to go in front.'

'You can if you map read,' said Jake, removing his jacket. He looked decidedly impatient as he waited for them all to board the Land Rover.

Tania settled herself in her seat, prepared for the long drive, and Max lurched against her as they set off. Out of the window she glimpsed low cloud on the distant hills. Near at hand the stone walls edging the fields looked dark grey and the occasional ash tree was stark against the sky. It looked surreal, something out of a mystery novel. She could hardly believe they were on their way at last.

'Where are we going?' asked one of the girls after a while.

Gregor swivelled round. 'Don't you know? We're going to walk up to the head of the Wharfe, and then on up to the watershed.'

'Watershed?'

'You'll see the place at the top where the becks flow in opposite directions down the hill, one to the North Sea and the other to the Irish Sea,' said Jake.

The girl looked perplexed. 'Why?'

'Because we'll have reached the high point in the Pennines.'

'You don't expect the becks to flow *up* the hill do you?' said Gregor scornfully.

The girl looked as if she didn't care where they flowed. Her face had lost its colour and she took a gulp of air.

'Are you all right?' Tania said. Stupid question. Of course she wasn't. She leant forward urgently. 'Jake, stop!'

He pulled into a gateway and yanked on the handbrake. 'Be quick,' he said, his voice sharp. 'We've not much time to spare.'

At once Tania was up and propelling the girl off the vehicle and out into the cold air. They were only just in time.

She waited until the spluttering stopped and then found a wad of tissues.

'Here, take these,' she said. 'I'm Tania, by the way.'

'Becky,' the girl said, shivering.

'Come on, Becky. Let's walk up and down a bit until you feel better.'

Backwards and forwards they went, slipping a little on the wet grass on the roadside and ignoring the waving from those in the Land Rover. Becky needed this and a few extra minutes would make no difference. The air smelt of cold but the freshness in it made Tania's face glow.

Jake's shoulders were hunched as they got back on board and he was frowning as if he suspected they had wasted time on purpose. Surely his determination to start this walk in good time wasn't of more importance than Becky being ill, she thought as they started off again. How callous was that?'

The scenery was wilder now they had left the trees behind. Sheets of barren moorland stretched away as far as Tania could see. They were climbing now and the hills in the far distance looked misty and remote. Today or tomorrow they would be walking over there, following the route that Jake had mapped out. A ripple of excitement stirred deep inside her. She couldn't wait to get going. *Florence, eat your heart out*, she thought with a smile. She would far rather be here.

'Are we nearly there?' asked Max.

'I think so,' Tania said.

She glanced round at Becky again and hoped she was right. The girl was leaning back, eyes closed and keeping quite still. Some of her colour had returned to her cheeks though, and that was a good sign.

'Will she be all right now?' the other girl, Collette, mouthed at Tania from across the aisle.

Tania nodded, hoping her optimism was well-founded. They were on a steep narrow road now with nowhere to pull in.

Come on, come on, come on, she urged silently.

At last Jake drove into a walled yard and parked near a group of buildings backed by evergreen trees. Laughing and talking, they all piled out and grabbed their luggage from the back of the vehicle, getting in each other's way as they did so.

'I'll not be long,' Jake said. 'I've some arrangements to make about leaving the vehicle here for our return, that's all.'

He slammed shut the rear door and marched off, his boots scraping on the cobbles. In his bulky walking gear, and with his huge rucksack hoisted high on his back, he looked supremely confident. The roll of sleeping bag slung across the top made him appear taller and broader than before.

'I'll never be able to carry my rucksack with all this stuff in it,' Collette said. She gave a mock groan as she staggered a few steps bent double. 'I hope Jake knows what he's doing.'

'Knows what he's doing about what?' Jake asked, rejoining them.

'Don't worry, we all trust you,' said Collette as she rammed her woolly hat over her abundant curly hair and grinned at him.

Gregor looked up quickly and as he did so a dog barked from behind the stone buildings to the left. Startled, he let go of the map he was holding and the wind lifted it so unexpectedly that it blew down over the wall into the beck beyond.

Jake climbed over to retrieve it and pulled it up dripping wet. 'You really are the limit, Gregor,' he said as he leapt back to join them.

Gregor glared at him. 'Why didn't you do something about it faster then?'

Ignoring him, Jake turned to the others. 'All ready?' He nodded in satisfaction at the response. 'Let's go.'

Tension Begins

They set off along the narrow path in a single line. The ground underfoot was springy at first and their footsteps made no sound.

'So, Tania,' Jake said from immediately behind her. 'We have you to thank for making this possible.'

She turned to look at him. 'I was afraid you would turn me down as unsuitable.'

'You did?'

The surprise in his voice sounded genuine. Maybe he didn't recognise her? 'Well, yes,' she said.

'I like a bit of spirit.'

She heard the smile in his voice and was aware that he knew exactly where he had first met her, lying at his feet in a pile of snow accusing him bitterly of condoning his protégé's loutish behaviour.

'On Gregor's part?'

'On yours.'

'I see.' She walked some way in silence, not knowing what to say.

'What are your interests, Tania?' he said after a while. 'What do you like doing? Tell me about yourself.'

A tall order. She hesitated, feeling a strong need to impress this man with qualities he'd value. Now what would they be? Winner of marathons, abseiling champion, leader of climbing expeditions in the Himalayas? Too bad she couldn't come out with anything like that.

She stole a swift look at his face as he glanced ahead to check that all was well. He was ultra-capable, definitely, and probably knew all that was needed for a venture like this. Her poor efforts wouldn't make much difference.

Her secretarial skills and interest in watercolour painting would hardly count. How about a dab hand at tobogganing down snowy hillsides? Hardly. Or the first prize she had got at the village photographic competition a year or two ago? That wouldn't do either.

'I don't take kindly to being disliked,' was all she could come out with.

He smiled again, briefly this time. 'Gregor's a good lad at heart.'

She was silent as she waited behind the boys to climb another stile. So far the boy had said or done nothing to make her change her bad opinion of him. He could be a real nuisance on a walk like this.

'Have you done this sort of thing before?' Jake said when they got going again, on rougher ground now.

'Parts of the Pennine Way, that sort of thing,' she said. 'But only by the day. My family did quite a bit of fell walking as I was growing up and I grew to love it. Max has always been keen too.'

'A long distance walk over several days is quite a different thing than going out by the day,' he said.

'Of course.'

'Psychologically it's a test of stamina.'

'I can understand that,' she said.

'It's not the distance involved that's the problem as much as the knowledge that you have to keep going day after day come what may and carry most of what you need with you.'

She was silent. Did he imagine she hadn't thought of that?

'We'll be going to some remote areas not reachable by road,' he said. 'We'll be on our own.'

'Annie explained all that.'

'Does it bother you?'

'Not a bit. I like the feeling of being self sufficient.'

'What about your brother? Will he cope?'

'Max?' She looked ahead to check on him again and saw him running in front of the girls.

'Stop!' Jake bawled with a suddenness that set Tania's heart thudding. 'Back here, lad, please.'

Max slid to a halt. 'I wasn't doing anything.'

'No running. The shale is loose here.

We don't want accidents.'

'He was all right,' said Tania quickly.

'He's my responsibility now. He'll do as I say.'

She could hardly bear to look at her brother's downcast face as he obeyed. Max was only nine. Surely he should be given some leeway?

'Map reading skills?' Jake said as if there had been no interruption.

'A bit,' she said.

'Cooking?'

She nodded.

'Anything else I should know?'

The track narrowed here between a stone wall on one side and an overgrown hawthorn hedge on the other. Collette, in front of Tania, let go of a branch that shot back and caught Tania on the side of her neck.

She flinched. 'Careful,' she warned.

To her surprise Jake made no comment. How unfair was that? One of the others, shorter than herself, could have been injured by getting the thorny branch full in the face.

'First aid?'

What's this, an interrogation?' she demanded.

Anxious to put distance between them she surged ahead to join Becky who was trudging along with her head down.

'OK, Becky?' Tania asked breathlessly.

The girl nodded. 'I'm tired.'

'Me too. But we'll be stopping to eat our lunch soon.'

'Why have you come with us, Tania?' Becky asked. 'And why did you bring your brother? Collette says he's only nine.'

By the time Tania explained the situation they had reached the top of an incline where a drystone wall gave shelter from the breeze.

'A brief lunch stop here,' said Jake.

Becky unzipped the top pocket of her rucksack and pulled out a packet of sandwiches. 'Gran made these,' she said with satisfaction. 'She always puts in masses of mayonnaise. I like mayonnaise.'

'You live with your grandmother?'

Becky's expression immediately closed up. 'Some of the time,' she muttered.

Tania bit her lip and glanced round to check if Jake had overheard. The expression on his face didn't change as he gazed thoughtfully into the distance.

Definitely breaking the rules on her part to question any of them on personal matters. Black mark.

'It's OK,' Becky muttered.

They set off again and Tania glanced at Gregor trudging stony-faced beside them. He didn't say anything so why should she have this feeling that he was planning something in secret that was going to make a big difference to them all?

Words of Comfort

By the time they reached a wooden building half-hidden by a belt of trees where they were to spend the night, they were all glad to climb the steps to the door and crowd into a small dark hallway that smelt musty as if no-one had been here for a long time.

'Boots off, everyone,' Jake commanded.

With cries of relief, rucksacks came off too and were dumped in whatever space was available. At once, before anyone had time to grumble, Jake allocated rooms. Then he nodded to Tania. 'I'll get a game or two organised outside while your team prepares the evening meal. Can you can cope?'

She threw back her head at the doubt in his voice. 'And who are my team?' she demanded. 'Or aren't I allowed to know that?'

He threw her an enigmatic look. 'I've a copy of the list here for you. Good enough?'

'Not quite. Do I rustle up a meal out of thin air?'

For answer he got out a large packet from his rucksack. It rattled a little as she took it from him. 'This is it,' he said. 'Just add boiling water and simmer for a while as you'll see.'

Tania looked at it in astonishment. 'Chicken Supreme,' she read out loud. 'I don't believe it.'

'There's rice, too, and apples for afterwards. Any problem with that?'

Bemused, Tania shook her head.

Afterwards Jake's team dealt with the washing up, leaving the crockery and cutlery on the table ready for breakfast next morning.

Then Collette and the boys went outside with him to kick a ball about while Tania and Becky inspected the rest of the packets of food that Jake had unearthed from his rucksack earlier.

'Muesli,' said Becky. 'I like that.'

44

'To have with powdered milk like we used in the tea,' Tania said. 'Oh, and here's bread and small packets of butter and jam too. At least we won't starve.'

She was surprised they had even that. More concerned about the route they would be taking, she hadn't thought to ask Annie what they were doing about food.

She stifled a huge yawn.

'Early bed, I think,' said Jake, returning at that moment.

When Tania checked a little while later she found that the girls had already chosen their beds in the room allocated to them. Both of them were in top bunks, she noticed, and fast asleep.

She spread out her sleeping bag on the lower deck of another bunk bed, sorted out her few belongings as quietly as she could and then returned to the main room where Jake was poring over an Ordnance Survey map.

'This is where we're heading for tomorrow,' he said, pointing to a spot on the map. His brow was furrowed and he gave the impression of intense concentration coupled with immense energy.

She knew he wanted these young people to be proud of their achievements in doing what demanded stamina and strength of mind as well as body. She resolved to do all she could to help.

Suddenly he looked up and his face relaxed into a smile. 'We've done well today. A few blisters, that's all. That young brother of yours is a goer, Tania.'

She smiled at his praise. 'He's enjoying it.'

'Fancy a hot drink?' he said, getting up. 'Then I shall hit the hay. We've a long day ahead of us tomorrow.'

They sat drinking their tea for some time. Jake showed her the log book he had started for their trip where he would note down the map references of where they had stopped for rests and any other detail he thought relevant. 'It acts as proof if anything untoward comes up,' he said as he snapped the book shut.

'We'd better make sure nothing does go wrong then, hadn't we?' she said.

'That's the spirit. Well, I'm off now.'

She wasn't long in following him. Just a quick look at the map that was all, to memorise some of the place names they would be encountering tomorrow. Gillerthwaite and Yarnwotten, Clearwell Dyke and Bulliwater.

A slither of anticipation ran through her at the remoteness of all and she lay awake for a while listening to the quiet breathing of her charges.

★   ★   ★

Quiet sobbing woke her. She reached for her torch and sat up. 'Becky, Collette?'

A gasp from Becky's bed was her answer. Tania flicked the beam of torchlight in the direction of the two top bunks. Then she was out of bed reaching for her jacket and shoes with the floorboards creaking beneath her feet as she stood up.

'Becky, tell me, what's wrong.'

'I wish . . . I wish I hadn't come.'

In the other bunk Collette stirred. In a moment she would be awake, too, if she didn't do something quickly.

'Becky,' she whispered. 'Come on. Let's go in the other room and talk.'

Another sob answered her, but the girl struggled up, pulling on her thick jacket over her pyjamas and feeling for her trainers in the light of Tania's torch.

Becky shivered as they went into the main room. 'I don't like it here.'

Tania looked about her, feeling helpless. Highlighting the bare walls and bleak furniture by switching on the main light would make things seem even more depressing. She had a better idea. 'Let's go outside,' she said.

Becky helped her turn the heavy key and pull the bolts across. Outside, faint starlight lightened the icy darkness a little. They found a wooden bench against the wall to sit on, made comfortable by one of the spare blankets Tania had picked up in the main room and brought out with her. The other two they wrapped round them for warmth.

Tania switched off her torch. 'That's better,' she said. 'People might think we're spies if they see any lights flickering about from here.'

Becky gave a trembling laugh.

Tania gazed up at the sky, not knowing what to say to help Becky. Homesickness was devastating because it seemed at the time that it would never end. She had only known it once when camping with a school friend's family in the south of France, but she had never forgotten the agony of feeling far away from home and desolate. Poor Becky had had a lot of sadness in her young life. No proper home either, by the sound of it.

She cleared her throat and the sound was loud in the quiet night.

'They wouldn't let us bring our mobiles with us,' said Becky, her voice quivering. 'I want to ring Gran to come and take me home.'

'Does she stay up all night, your gran?'

'She'd come, I know she would.'

'My dad wouldn't,' said Tania.

Becky gave a shiver of surprise. 'Why not?'

'He'd go mad if I woke him up from his beauty sleep. But I bet your gran doesn't need any of that.'

'They wouldn't really think we're spies, would they, if they saw the torchlight?' Becky said after a short silence.

'Who knows? Even now someone might be peering out of their bedroom window wondering what we're up to.'

'But there aren't any houses.'

'So there aren't. It needs someone with a bit of common sense round here to notice that. I'm glad you're in my team, Becky.'

'Me too.'

'I'll tell you what, how about getting back to bed now and phoning your gran in the morning on my mobile?'

'You'd let me?'

'This is an emergency, isn't it? That what our mobiles are for, Jake's and mine. Good idea or what?'

'Thanks,' Becky muttered, getting to her feet.

As Tania stood up and turned to gather up the blankets she thought she saw a movement in the shadow by the door. Maybe the relief that Becky had agreed to her suggestion was making her see things that weren't there.

* * *

Jake stood in the shadow of the door. A sudden wish to breathe in the moorland air before sleeping had got him out of bed and out here late as it was. He had been surprised to see the two figures seated on the bench.

A faint murmuring of Tania's voice reached him and then Becky's in response. He could hear enough to be aware that their conversation would be spoilt by the presence of another. Tania was handling herself well in dealing with Becky's homesickness. A clumsy fool getting in on the act would not help in the slightest.

Becky was the newest recruit to the group he organised activities for at the weekends. There were one or two like-minded people who gave up their time willingly to help these young people recover from a variety of traumatic experiences. It usually fell to him to lead the kind of adventurous activity he had enjoyed when growing up.

He and an older woman experienced in fell walking had come up with the idea of a four-night walk at the half term break in February, something they hadn't tried before. Louise's enthusiasm was catching and he had put some plans in motion at once. Four was the sensible number of young people to take part and lots were drawn from those who seemed interested with the promise that everyone would get a chance to do a similar thing in due course.

Louise's disappointment was acute

when she had to pull out at the last minute. Becky was the one who nearly changed her mind about coming at that moment and it was only her friend, Collette's, scorn that stopped her. Jake wondered now if that had been the right decision.

The hazy starlight cast a faint glow over the night scene. He was glad to see that they had brought blankets out with them because the air was chill.

The bench creaked a little and he heard a muffled laugh, hastily extinguished. Silently he slipped back inside the building. Back in his room he listened for the sound of the bolt being pulled across on the door, and hearing it, got inside his sleeping bag. All was well here in the bunkhouse.

He stared up through the darkness, in his mind seeing the layout of the building and wondering, as he always did, what improvements might be made.

Whoever had done the barn conversion hadn't done a bad job but by throwing together his room and the one the boys occupied there might have been room for more beds so that larger groups could be accommodated.

But perhaps not. He was far too critical. But he had this urge always to improve on what was there and give it a new life. Rather like improving the lives of these youngsters he worked with in his spare time, giving them a taste of adventure and the knowledge that anything was possible if they had the courage to go for it. Or more or less anything.

He was only too aware that this was a huge responsibility, but the powers-that-be trusted his aims and his ability to look after these kids. And now he had an even younger lad with them. His eyes had been on Max most of the day and he had noted his determination to keep up with the rest. It seemed he liked a challenge and that was good.

All he needed was to be allowed to get on with it without being fussed over by his big sister or the others would have a field day if he didn't take care. Already he had seen the glint in Gregor's eyes at the prospect of a little fun at the lad's expense.

The first day had gone moderately well. For a time Louise's accident had almost doomed the project but then his fairy-godmother-cousin had waved her magic wand on their behalf and produced her best friend, Tania.

So far it seemed she might prove her worth, but there were plenty of difficult challenges ahead of them when her qualities of quick sympathy and of being a loyal friend might not be enough.

But they were here now and for the moment that was sufficient. He yawned, turned over and settled down to sleep.

★　★　★

Jake's group, on breakfast duty, had dumped the bag of cereal and a sliced loaf on the table ready for action by the time Tania appeared next morning.

Collette, her curly hair tousled and

her face flushed with the exertion, was filling the huge black kettle at the sink.

'That's heavy,' said Tania. 'Let me help. Where's everybody?'

Collette looked vague as she handed the kettle over. 'Outside, I think.'

'Becky?'

'Doing a job for Jake. One of the boys ran off somewhere and she's gone to get him back.'

Tania's heart lurched. Max? This didn't sound good.

She carried the kettle to the stove, found the matches and lit the gas. 'Guard this, Collette. Turn it off when it boils.'

She went outside into the gloomy morning and heard shouts and the scurry of footsteps coming from the other side of the building.

To her relief Max appeared, pushing and shoving to get past Gregor. No problem there then, she thought as she went inside with them.

Jake was looking at his watch. 'Get a move on, everybody,' he ordered.

'But where's Becky?' asked Tania. 'And Wayne?'

Jake threw her an unfathomable look. 'Two from your group, Tania. Isn't that so?'

She stared back at him. 'As you well know.'

'Becky was up early today, all bright and shining.'

'I'm glad to hear it.'

She joined the others at the long wooden table. By the time they were all served Becky came in with Wayne, red-eyed, behind her. Another homesick one, Tania thought in sudden pity. Jake, though, merely indicated the two empty spaces with a nod of his head.

Tania wondered at his calmness in view of something that could be a problem. Was there nothing Jake didn't cope with in that calm way of his, his assumption that all would be well making it happen? That must be what made him appear so ultra-confident, she thought.

'Pass the cereal, you greedy lot,' said Becky. 'I'm starving.'

Tania looked at her in surprise. Was this the girl who had been a quivering mass of emotion in the middle of the night? Looking up she caught Jake's intent gaze on her and felt her cheeks burn. He must have heard some sound last night and come out to check on them. It was surprising that he hadn't made his presence known or interfered in her handling of the situation.

She wondered what her reaction would have been if he had insisted on taking over. But she was glad he hadn't or Becky might not have opened up to her and the right words might not have spilled out of her mouth of their own volition and satisfied the girl. Her gamble on offering her mobile had paid off, it seemed.

But she hated the feeling of being watched and judged by this man whose opinion of her was already at rock bottom.

A Difficult Time

When at last they were ready, Jake set off at a smart pace. They reached the road, walked along it for a while and then climbed a stile to take a path that led through a farmyard.

She heard the murmuring of voices and the movement of an animal in one of the barns. Once out onto open fell on the other side, Jake paused to point out a swathe of low cloud in the distance that hid the summit of Galderpot.

Gregor groaned. 'You won't catch me climbing that.'

'Please yourself,' said Jake pleasantly. 'You're welcome to join the rest of us as we skirt round it on the track that leads up to Gillerthwaite.'

Gregor hunched his shoulders, kicked a stone out his way, but said nothing.

'It sounds dreadful,' said Wayne,

turning to look back at Tania.

'It's not that far really,' Tania said. 'If you were a bird, like that buzzard up there, you'd fly there in no time.'

'Buzzard?' said Wayne, stopping suddenly. 'Where?'

Tania stopped too. 'You're interested in birds?'

'I've brought my bird book. I'll show you.' He tried to shrug his shoulders out of the straps of his rucksack.

'Not now, lad,' Jake ordered. 'We've got to get on.'

Flushing, Wayne pulled on his rucksack again and then stumbled a little in his haste to catch up with the others. The way they were travelling was now a faint track, sometimes a sheep path and sometimes almost hidden as they pressed on one behind the other over the coarse, wet moorland grass that smelt of wet earth.

Tania bit her lip and shot a furious look at Jake's back as he strode ahead. Wayne was a game little lad. Why couldn't Jake have been more understanding and allowed him a minute or two to get his book out? The man was such a strange mixture of compassion and sternness.

They reached Gillerthwaite after a couple of hours, a small collection of grey stone cottages and a village shop nestling into the hillside. The village church was on the outskirts, behind a band of leafless trees.

'A short rest, I think,' said Jake.

Tania smiled at the murmur of relief from everyone. She was pleased, too, to be able to stop for a while to ease her aching feet.

'I'm going to the shop to buy something,' said Gregor, pulling a handful of change from his pocket and jingling it.

'Feel free,' said Jake. 'Three inside at a time or we'll crowd the place out and Miss Crabbe won't like it. Tania and Max can go in with you.'

Tania followed her eager brother into the dim interior that made it hard to see anything at first, but the smell of beeswax mixed with a slight hint of paraffin was welcoming. When her eyes became accustomed to the gloom she saw a small elderly lady in a mauve jersey smiling at her from behind the wooden counter.

'You'll be the Anderson party who ordered the packed lunches,' she said. 'I have them all ready for you and the rest of the things you wanted.'

'Thank you,' said Tania, marvelling at Jake's forethought. She had to hand it to him. His organising skills were first class even if his peremptory manner sometimes got her back up. She smiled. 'Jake's outside,' she said. 'He's in charge and he'll be in for them in a minute. He's guarding the others and only allowing us in three at a time.'

Miss Crabbe looked approving. 'Such a considerate one always thinking of others.'

'He's been here before?'

'Aye, I knew him when he was just a young lad. I was glad to see him again a few weeks back when he came to make arrangements for today. He hasn't changed, still the young gentleman.'

'But a bit taller?'

Miss Crabbe's eyes twinkled. 'Aye, lass, just a bit. The lady with him was tall too and very kind to an old woman.'

Lady? This would be the person who had to pull out of the walk because of her injured ankle, Tania thought. Probably as competent as he was himself. What a let-down for him having to put up with her inadequacies instead!

'Look, Tania, kittens,' said Max gazing up at her with such pleasure that her heart was touched.

Gregor, his purchases paid for, knelt on the floor beside him to stroke the soft fur of the little ginger and white creatures curled up in a basket watched over by their friendly mother.

'I want one,' he said.

Their owner smiled. 'They're too young to leave their mother yet awhile, lad.'

Jake was last into the shop and a few moments later and Miss Crabbe followed him outside. She looked from one to the other doubtfully. 'You'll take care?' she said. 'There was a bad weather forecast on the radio earlier.'

'Then we'll get on at once,' said Jake. 'And thank you again, Miss Crabbe. Come on, everyone, get moving.'

By the time Jake called a halt for lunch they had reached a rock-strewn river that rippled its way through a narrowing dale where boulders were strewn about on the river bank. These made good seats and Tania chose one a little apart from the rest and then checked to see where Max was.

'You can take your eyes off your brother for a minute or two,' said Jake, seating himself near her.

She hunched her shoulders, annoyed at his words. 'I'm making sure he's OK, that's all.'

'No favouritism, please.'

'That's not fair.'

'You think not?'

'He's nine years old, a little lad and I have to look after him.'

'Why? You think he's incapable of

mixing in with the rest without you bossing him about. Give him a chance, Tania.'

How dare he criticise the way she looked after Max! She bit back a sharp retort with difficulty and felt like leaping up and wiping that superior expression from his tanned face. Only the presence of the youngsters stopped her. If Jake's eagle eye was going to be on her every time she looked at Max the next few days would be a nightmare.

Suddenly Jake sprang to his feet. 'Stop that, Gregor!' he bawled.

Startled, Tania looked across to where Gregor was poised on a boulder leaning over the water. At Jake's command he jumped back onto the river bank and then moved away from the river and threw himself down on the ground with his back to the rest of them.

'Can you hear that?' said Collette suddenly. 'Something's mewing like a kitten. Listen!'

'It *is* a kitten,' said Becky, round-eyed.

Tania got up and moved across to Gregor's discarded rucksack and undid the top buckle. Even before she had fully loosened the strings she saw the tiny ginger and white body inside. Gently she lifted it out. 'Look!' she breathed.

The kitten screwed up its tiny eyes against the light.

'Gregor, over here at once!' Jake thundered. 'What's the meaning of this?'

Tania held the kitten close to her face, smoothing its soft fur with one finger. It was so tiny, so helpless.

'Its mum'll miss it,' said Max, his mouth turned down at the corners.

Gregor glared at the kitten and then rushed down to the river again. 'Leave me be, the lot of you!'

Jake leapt after him, caught hold of him by the shoulder and dragged him away from the edge. 'Don't move,' he ordered. 'This has got to be sorted.'

The others stood in a tight bunch to see what would happen and the atmosphere was electric.

Tania had had enough. She glared at Jake and felt her face flood with warmth. 'Leave this to me and don't interfere,' she commanded. 'I'm dealing with this. I'm taking the poor little thing back to Miss Crabbe. Don't wait for me. I'll catch you up.'

For a moment, unbelievably, Jake recognised dread in those grey eyes of hers. Surely she wasn't afraid of what he would do with the kitten?

Deep in thought he watched Tania stride off until she was out of sight and then turned his attention to the girls and boys in his care.

Learning About Jake

The second day on a long-distance trail was always tricky because the euphoria of setting out was beginning to wear off. And Gregor's stroppy behaviour was definitely over the top. He would have to watch him closely for the rest of the time or there might be real trouble after the traumatic events the poor lad had had to deal with lately.

On the whole, though, they were doing well even with a young lad like Max in the party. He hoped that by now Tania understood the importance of completing the challenge and the pride in a successful outcome gave these youngsters a sense of their own worth that was invaluable to their wellbeing. Fussing over her brother was not on.

He raised his head to look at the far hills ahead of them. They were hidden in cloud now and no birds soared in the darkening sky. Miss Crabbe had warned them of bad weather to come. He raised his head and sniffed the air. Definitely an added chill to it and he didn't like the look of those clouds. He hoped Tania wouldn't be long.

'How about creating a way of crossing the river here while we wait?' he suggested. 'Come on you lot, don't be beaten. See how much you can do in ten minutes. I'm timing you now.'

There were groans from some, but Collette leapt up at once, keen to see if it could be done.

'What's the point?' Gregor said and then obeyed with alacrity as Jake took a step towards him.

To Jake's approval they worked as a team, collecting rocks of a size and shape to make firm stepping stones. Gregor was first across, shouting out his triumph so that Tania, hurrying back up the track towards them, obviously heard and quickened her pace.

Jake's surge of relief and pleasure at

seeing her took him by surprise.

'She's back!' Collette cried.

He smiled as they all clustered round him, prepared to set off again. Tania had acted at once and saved a difficult situation. He was pleased she had it in her. Her answering smile cheered him. In it he imagined a sense of comradeship, a willingness to pull together and the determination to succeed.

★ ★ ★

The way back to Gillerthwaite had seemed long. She had been walking on soft turf beside the river to start with and the water bubbled pleasantly over its rock-strewn bed. Tania, cradling the small soft body of the kitten in her hands, felt the weight of responsibility to get the tiny thing back to its mother as quickly as possible.

Thank goodness Collette had heard the tiny thing mewing in Gregor's rucksack before they had gone even further. She couldn't begin to imagine what a thug of a boy like Gregor thought he was doing unless a sadistic streak in him had inspired the stupid act. For a startled moment a vulnerable expression had flicked across Jake's strong features and she had felt the need to take charge at once and sort out this problem for him. Now she felt amazed at her daring.

She came to the stone bridge, crossed it to the other side and before long her path lead to the lane leading down to the village, a welcome short cut.

Ignoring their previous route she hurried on, remembering the look of wonder on Gregor's face as he knelt in Miss Crabbe's shop to peer into the basket of kittens. That wasn't the expression of a boy bent on mischief. He had looked dreamy as he rubbed his fingers gently over the soft body and she had seen a new side to someone she had obviously judged too harshly. That was what Jake obviously recognised in him and wished to encourage.

Humbled, she arrived at the shop and opened the door. The bell jangled and there was Miss Crabbe smiling kindly at her.

'I had to come back,' Tania said a little breathlessly. 'I've brought the kitten back to its mother.'

Unsurprised, Miss Crabbe gazed at the tiny body in Tania's hands. Then she smiled and took it from her to place beside its mother. There were rustlings in the basket and a gentle mewing.

'It'll do right well now, lass,' Miss Crabbe said.

'You'd missed it?'

'The mother couldn't settle. She's glad it's back.'

'Me too,' said Tania fervently. 'Jake's sorry about it. We all are.'

'He's fond of animals, is Mr Anderson. He had a dog as a young lad, a terrier of some sort. He and his brother thought the world of it. But when his brother died the dog went too. I often wondered.'

Tania was shocked. 'His brother *died*?'

'Aye, lass. He was the eldest by a good few years. They came this way often before that, the Anderson family. But never after that.'

'You've been here a long time?' Tania asked, her mind still on the tragedy.

'My parents' shop. And I carried on here after them. Sit down for a minute, lass. You look right pale.'

'No, no, I must get back. They're waiting for me.'

Tania rushed out, aware of her brusqueness, but unable to stay there a moment longer. Annie had never told her of this tragedy in her family but perhaps it had happened before she was born, many years ago when Miss Crabbe's parents had kept the shop and Miss Crabbe had been young herself.

★   ★   ★

'You've done this before, Gregor, haven't you?' Tania said, as she walked beside him.

'What if I have?'

'Just asking. So you'd like a kitten of your own?'

He shrugged. 'What do I want a kitten for?'

'Something to look after, to love?'

'I look after myself,' said Gregor. He kicked a stone on the path with a viciousness that was alarming. It shot into the rough grass.

'I'm glad I wasn't in the way of that,' said Tania.

He shot her a scornful look. 'That's nothing. I can kick harder than that.'

She could well believe it and kept a careful watch out as they moved across the rough ground, prepared to leap out of the way of his ill temper if need be.

After a while their path left the river bank. They were climbing steadily now to join another path that wound over the brow of a hill.

Down in the hollow ahead of them was a large group of stone buildings so well camouflaged that they seemed settled into the bare fell on which they stood. With Gregor at the rear they straggled down the track to the porch where three dogs got up slowly to greet them. Jake thumped on the door. It opened immediately.

'Aye, you're the folk for the bunkhouse,' a deep Yorkshire voice announced. A grin spread across the man's rugged features. 'Aye, I saw you coming. I didn't have the heart to tell you the bunkhouse is out of order.'

'Out of order?' shrieked Collette 'You mean we can't stay here?'

'My fun,' he said laconically.

'Fun!' Collette spluttered.

'Mr Thwaite?' asked Jake. 'You're expecting us, I believe?'

'Aye, Bill Thwaite of Slough Fell. I'll get the key.'

He reached up to a hook for it and then pulled on heavy boots and a long jacket. 'Follow me,' he said. He whistled for one of the dogs, a large black and white collie. 'Here, Aussie. Good lad.'

He led them across a yard and up a

track to a building they could see in the distance.

'It's a long way,' grumbled Gregor, keeping well away from the dog.

'Just a quarter of a mile, lad,' he said. 'A dull day for walking and worse brewing.'

Jake frowned. 'We had a warning back there. Snow, do you think?'

Bill Thwaite winked at Tania. 'Could be.'

She tried to smile back though the skin on her face felt tight with exhaustion. Jake had been hard on them, keeping up a cracking pace all day. The only surprise was that he had been content for them all to wait for her while she returned the kitten. She had imagined running for miles to catch them up, but when she got back he had given her a look of appreciation. That was one good mark in his favour anyway, but she wasn't convinced that he would approve of her for long.

The farmer went first up some rough steps and thrust the key into the lock.

The door creaked open.

'I'll not stop,' he said. 'Plenty to do with getting the sheep down from the tops. If you want owt you know where to find me. Mobiles are useless up here.'

Then he was gone.

Inside, the air struck chill. Becky, the first in, gave a strangled scream as she nearly went flying over something stacked in the passage. 'A spade and shovel!' she cried in protest.

'A booby trap?' said Gregor, sounding interested.

'One minute,' said Jake, feeling for the light switch.

Dazzled, Tania moved towards a door at the end. The large room on the other side felt cold. A couple of long sagging sofas almost filled two of the walls, and what room was left was filled with upright chairs and a wooden bench. The table in the middle of the room was piled high with maps and leaflets in untidy piles.

Jake was busy at one of the electric

heaters, fiddling with the knobs. 'Heat!' he said in satisfaction as a red glow appeared.

They gathered round it.

Stern Words

When their charges were getting ready for bed later, Tania sat at the wooden table exhausted in mind and body. She stretched her legs out to ease the aching muscles in her calves and tried hard not to allow her eyelids to droop. Jake, opposite, looked as drained as she felt herself.

'We'll have a good few miles to cover tomorrow,' he said.

Tania managed not to groan. She thought of Ivan beneath Italian skies and of the crowds of sightseers enjoying all that Florence could offer. So vastly different from here. What was she doing tramping through barren wastes with a leader who thought more about pride in achievement than human need? Surely he should consider the enjoyment of his charges too?

A small sigh escaped her and she

coughed to cover it.

She felt Jake's penetrating gaze on her like a laser beam. 'Something wrong?' he asked.

'Nothing,' she said with a firmness she hoped was convincing.

'I'm glad to hear it.'

Nothing was wrong that a good night's sleep in a warm bed wouldn't cure, she thought. Or better still a comfortable four star hotel in some fabulously warm place.

He quirked an eyebrow. 'Something amusing you?'

'Not really,' she said, at once back in her present surroundings in which there was nothing funny at all.

From one of the bedrooms came the sounds of yelling and Jake got to his feet to investigate. 'And neither is that sort of racket,' he said, striding to the door.

After a few moments he returned and slumped down in his seat. 'Your turn next, Tania, if there is a next time.'

A shriek split the air.

'That's Max!' she cried leaping up.

She found her brother cowering on one of the top bunks of the boys' room. Gregor was swinging his sleeping bag round his head. 'Look out, I'm coming to get you!'

'What are you doing?' Tania cried.

'None of your business.'

'Leave him alone, you bully.'

'What's going on?' demanded Jake from behind her. 'Gregor, put that down and behave yourself.'

Tania turned swiftly. 'He's attacking my brother.'

'Just a bit of fun,' mumbled Gregor.

'All right, Max?' said Jake.

Max nodded, his face so pale that Tania wanted to take him in her arms and hug him. With a glance at Jake she took a step back.

'Get back to bed, Gregor, and the rest of you. Keep your fun and games for tomorrow,' Jake ordered.

'Mummy's boy, mummy's boy,' Gregor sang softly as he climbed up to the top of another bunk.

Tania stood a furious step towards him, but before she knew it Jake had grabbed hold of her and propelled into the main room, slamming the door shut behind them.

She turned on him, feeling the blood surge to her head. He caught her to him and held her fast against his rough jersey, breathing deeply. She wanted to lash out at him. Her helplessness was humiliating.

'Calm yourself, Tania,' he said. 'You're over-reacting.'

'Over-reacting?' she cried. How else would she react at such spiteful words? Max had been so brave after his initial outburst when the news had come from the hospital even though deep down he was devastated at the loss of their mother. He didn't deserve cruel taunts from a boy who should have known better.

She took several deep breaths before pulling free at last still trembling a little and unable to say any more.

'Get things in proportion,' Jake said,

his voice sharp. 'And life will be easier for all of us.'

Tears sprang to her eyes and she brushed her hand across her face, ashamed of her weakness. He seemed to tower over her and, still shaking she took a step away from him.

'The girls are quiet now. You'd best get to bed,' he said gruffly.

He turned away from her, his shoulders hunched. Nothing more to be said, she thought, exhausted.

Sleep was long in coming. She thought of Max curled up in his bunk, unhappy because of Gregor's bullying and of Dad alone at home believing his young son was having the time of his life on an adventure holiday dear to his heart.

It was like a pain this feeling of powerlessness because she didn't know what to do except to keep a strict eye on Gregor and try to keep Max away from him.

She had to face the fact that Jake was in charge and Jake didn't understand Max at all.

Cause for Concern

Last night the ceiling above her bunk had looked dull and grimy. On waking this morning it was gleaming with a strange light that made Tania leap up in bed and look round the room in wonder.

Everything shone with a brightness that hadn't been there before. She slid out of bed, shivering. The ledge outside was piled so high she could hardly see out of the window. Snow must have been falling for hours for it to be so deep, and it was still snowing.

Her spirit leapt to see it and she felt in the pocket of her rucksack for her camera. She wanted to be out there, revelling in the beauty and feeling the strange excitement snow always gave her. But no, she must be sensible. With no-one else awake she would get dressed and start things moving and prove to Jake she wasn't the helpless wimp he thought she was.

The air in the big room seemed musty as well as cold. She rattled the curtains back from the window. Warmth was needed immediately and she moved away to turn on the nearest heater. Nothing, not even the faintest plopping sound or from the other one either. She tried the light switch. The power was off. There was nothing else for it but to thump on the door of Jake's room and announce the bad news.

Jake was out at once, pulling his thick jersey on over his track suit and smoothing back his unruly hair. 'No power?'

'I can't get the heaters to light.'

He tried too without success. 'This is bad,' he said as he straightened.

She shivered. 'We can't boil the kettle either.'

'Maybe the farm's luckier. We'll need to find out.'

'Now?'

'Why not? We'll starting clearing

outside while everyone's warm in bed.'

He pulled his jacket, waterproof trousers and boots on quickly as she did too. He turned the key in the outside door and gave a hard yank. 'Something's stuck,' he said. 'Hand me the spade, Tania.'

She passed it to him and picked up the small shovel for herself. He yanked the door open and started to dig a way through the snow that had piled up against it.

The icy air caught at Tania's throat and crisp snow crunched beneath her feet. Jake worked hard to clear a few steps and then paused.

'I'll go first with the spade while you clear around the door and the steps,' he ordered. 'We don't want anyone falling over and getting hurt. When you've done that follow me and take over while I get my breath back. At least it's stopped snowing now.'

Twenty minutes later Tania's face glowed and life was coming back into her limbs.

'Everything looks the same,' she said when it was her turn to take over with the spade. 'You can't see where the cloud ends and the land begins.'

She dug fiercely for a while and then stopped to ease her back. Jake was standing upright and holding the shovel in one hand.

'A white-out,' he said.

'White-out?'

'That's when shadows don't exist because the cloud cover seems to merge with the snow. You can't see the horizon because of the reflecting and refracting of the glare and you've no idea how close it is. In certain conditions this can be dangerous.'

'I can imagine,' she said.

'It's like white night. You can't pick out anything on the surface unless it's large and dark.'

'Like the bunkhouse?'

'Yes, that. If we were further away it would seem to loom through the mist at us.'

'Eerie.'

'You could say that.'

He smiled briefly and the look they exchanged seemed full of complicity she found cheering. The silence surrounding them was no longer eerie, but seemed full of promise. They seemed the only people in this strange white world.

He cleared his throat. 'I owe you an apology.'

She looked at him in surprise, silenced by his intense expression.

'You've done well, Tania, coming with us at the last moment, dealing with everything thrown at you.'

'I've tried to do my best.'

'I'm afraid I over-reacted yesterday evening.'

Light dawned. 'When Gregor bullied Max?'

'I should have dealt with it differently, remembered your brother's young age and acted accordingly. Gregor's had so much trouble in his life that he needs specialist handling and I'm aware I don't have that. Sometimes I try too hard.'

Jake's eyes looked troubled and she was touched by his sudden vulnerability. 'But you do so much for him, for them all,' she said.

'I try but it's not always enough.'

'But how would it be for him if you did nothing?'

He straightened his shoulders. 'There's that, I suppose. But I want more than anything to help that boy come to terms with his past and to know he has some sort of future.'

'And the others too?'

He smiled. 'Of course. You have a way of seeing clearly, Tania, and I'm sorry your brother was in the way.'

She nodded, suddenly overcome by the tears welling in her throat. She felt privileged now to have the opportunity to be here with them all.

Warmed by this she worked even harder, thinking that the snow glittered more beautifully now than she could have imagined. She felt bemused and shaken by their apparent closeness. Working together like this felt good.

She knew she could trust Jake to overcome any obstacle and the knowledge of that sent a warm glow through her that was wonderful.

He shot her a look of approval and her heart soared.

'We'd better check if anyone else is up,' he said at last. 'Leave the tools here, Tania. We'll get two teams organised. They're bound to be stirring by now.'

She straightened, easing her back. As they got close to the bunkhouse the door opened and Wayne burst out, waving.

'Keep the door shut,' Jake called. 'You're letting the cold in.'

'Gregor's gone,' Wayne shouted back at him, panic in his voice. 'He's not in his room.'

A Problem Solved

'You're sure that you've looked absolutely everywhere, Wayne?'

Wayne nodded, looking scared. 'He's gone.'

Shocked, Tania gazed round at the white scene. They had seen no footprints other than their own when they had come out here to start clearing snow so Gregor must have left before it started.

The same thought occurred to Jake. His face paled. 'Let's get inside. Has he taken anything with him, his rucksack? Check that, will you, Wayne, while I work out what's to be done.'

'But how did he get out?' Tania said. 'The key was in the lock.'

Jake looked at her in surprise. 'So it was.'

She was breathless suddenly and her legs felt weak. Suppose it had been Max who was out there in that white wilderness, lost and cold and not knowing how to get back?

Suddenly she remembered the draught from the kitchen window and rushed to look.

'That's how Gregor got out,' she said. 'The catch was loose and he pushed the window closed after him so no-one would notice.'

Jake stared at the window, his lips tight.

The girls emerged their rooms, rubbing their eyes. Max appeared too and the frightened excitement in the air deepened as Jake announced Gregor's disappearance.

'No doubt he's at the farmhouse gorging himself in the warm so don't get too worried,' he said, his voice light though Tania sensed the effort this took. 'Food first for us here before we get over there ourselves. Get stuck in, everyone. Cold milk to drink, and there's plenty of bread and cereal.'

They rushed to obey.

'And then pack your belongings as quickly as you can,' he ordered. 'We'll need to move on away from here as soon as we find him.'

'In these dreadful conditions?' Tania asked. The snow was deep and it looked as if more was coming.

'We'll check how bad it is first.'

She looked at him in surprise, wondering at his optimism. Not long before he had talked of the whiteout and how dangerous it could be. Didn't he realise that nothing had changed?

'At least the lad had the sense to take his rucksack with him,' he said.

'But not to unlock the door and escape through it.'

'That's not Gregor's way.'

'If he's at the farmhouse stuffing himself wouldn't Bill Thwaite welcome us there too?'

Jake ignored her words. 'Get your team organised to clear up in here, Tania, while the rest of us carry on with snow clearing.'

The subdued excitement in the air

was urging everyone on. Tania followed the members of her group out into the crisp air tasting the icy sweetness of it as the heavy door shut behind her.

Collette had found three boards nailed to wooden handles behind one of the sofas, perfect for snow-clearing. With that and the spade and the small shovel they worked at a fast rate, each team able to rest for a few minutes until it was their turn again. Soon the crisp snow became too tempting to those longing to put it to good use.

'Stop that!' Jake commanded as a snowball skimmed his head at the first changeover. 'Rest while you've got the chance, Collette.'

'Must we?' Max objected.

'Definitely. There might well be time later to play, I shouldn't wonder, but this is serious.'

'A matter of life or death?' Collette asked, interested.

'Enough of that,' said Jake. 'We've work to do. Get a move on, everybody.'

When it was her turn to hand over

her board, Tania straightened and stretched. She rubbed her icy nose, remembering what Jake had said about the white-out that made people do strange things from being disorientated.

Suppose Gregor had set off last night, got some way before the snow started and then as it got rapidly worse become completely lost? Would they find him at the farm as Jake supposed?

Jake paused in his strenuous exertions and handed the spade to Tania. 'The house in sight now,' he said.

She swung round and saw the low stone farmhouse and its surrounding cluster of barns and outhouses. The relief was enormous.

Moisture shone on Jake's forehead. Although he hadn't voiced any deep concern about Gregor's disappearance she knew he must surely be worried.

'I can see someone,' said Collette. 'The farmer. He's waving at us.'

'Phone's down and the electric's gone,' Bill Thwaite said when they reached him.

'We've a lad missing,' said Jake. 'Have you seen him?'

Bill scratched his head, the lines on his forehead deepening. 'He'll not get far in this. Sheltering in one of the laithes, barns, like as not. My lads are out clearing down to the barn at the back so we can get the tractor out and feed to the lambing yews down yonder. The wife's none too good. Baby not due for nigh on two months. I'm right worried.'

'Mrs Thwaite's ill?' said Tania, white-lipped.

'Nowt that won't be cured, like as not, if she takes things easy.'

Tania nodded though she wondered at his calm in the face of something that could turn to tragedy. But not always, she reminded herself, and not usually.

'You others stick around in the yard and keep out of the way.' Jake ordered. 'Tania, come with me.'

He grabbed the spade and set to work on clearing a path to the nearest building.

Anxiety for the boy seemed to give Tania extra strength and she knew Jake felt the same by the speed he was working. The wind was blowing harder now, whipping the loose snow into drifts. She shivered. 'Suppose Gregor's lying injured somewhere?'

Jake looked grim. 'He chose to leave the bunkhouse. No-one forced him.'

His words sounded heartless, but there was an edge to them that confirmed desperate concern.

A dog barked and Tania raised her head.

The barking increased into frenzy as Jake wrenched the door of the building open.

'It's Aussie,' Tania said shakily. 'He's guarding something,'

'Here boy!' called Jake, and the dog, sprang towards them, tail wagging.

Tania knelt to inspect the rucksack. 'It's Gregor's,' she said, marvelling. 'So he can't be far away.'

Aussie came outside with them and looked at them, bright-eyed. Then he stiffened, his nose pointing ahead to where another barn stood as the land dipped away into the misty distance.

Jake gave a shout, his voice carrying in the bitter air. 'Gregor, where are you?'

A faint cry answered him. Before they could stop him the dog bounded off towards the open door of the building, his body sharp against the snow. With his tail wagging triumphantly he ran to something in the straw that covered the floor.

'Get him off me!' Gregor cried as he staggered to his feet.

Jake grabbed the dog's collar and held it fast. 'It's all right, lad. I've got him. I won't let him near you.'

'Oh Gregor,' Tania cried, weak with relief. 'What were you doing, going off like that? It doesn't make sense.'

'Makes sense to me,' he muttered.

'Get a move on, Gregor,' said Jake. 'It's cold.'

'I am doing,' Gregor muttered. White-faced and shivering he edged away from the dog.

Snow was starting to fall again now and they met the rest of the group heading for the house.

'Bill said to go in and get warm while this lasts,' Collette said, shivering.

There was a stamping of boots in the porch and a collective sigh of relief as they started peeling off boots and hats and gloves.

Bill Thwaite followed them in, shutting the door on his dogs. Tania smiled at him, liking his rough exterior as he stood there in his filthy greatcoat. 'Aussie helped us find Gregor,' she said.

'That dog's good with people, not sheep,' Bill said.

'Why's he called Aussie?' asked Max.

'Father was an Australian dog, lad, brought over by a sheepshearer one season. Things are different over there. He's no use to me with his father's genes in him and bred not to work with the sheep till he's a two-year-old. I'll need to get rid of him.'

'Poor Aussie,' said Max.

Bill looked at Gregor, slumped against the protective bar of the Aga. 'That lad needs a shower.'

'Is there hot water?' asked Jake.

'Aye, the Aga's run on oil. I'll show the lad. I need to check on the wife. Then it's hot drinks.'

'Go on, Gregor,' said Jake, taking the rucksack from Tania and handing it to him.

'And Mrs Thwaite?' asked Tania when Bill came down again. 'How is she? Can I do anything for her?'

Bill shrugged and nodded towards the staircase. 'Aye, lass. Go on up. She'll want to see you.'

'You're a Bully'

Tania took a deep breath and then went slowly upstairs unsure of how the mistress of the house would react on seeing her or how she would find her. With great care she pushed open the bedroom door and peered inside. 'Mrs Thwaite?'

The patient was struggling to sit up in bed with a tartan blanket round her shoulders, obviously concerned about the activity going on in her kitchen below.

'Come in, lass. Nowt to be afraid of. You look right pale.'

'How are you, Mrs Thwaite?'

'A bit of a fraud lying here when there's work to be done. Bill shouldn't have let you stay in that old bunkhouse last night with bad weather coming in. He and our lads need to get things sorted outside in all this snow. I'll come down now and get things going.'

'No, no,' said Tania, alarmed. 'You stay right where you are, Mrs Thwaite. That's the orders. We can cope down there.'

'Are you sure, lass?'

Tania felt more confident now. 'Bill's making hot drinks for everyone. I'll bring one up for you in a minute. Hot water bottles?'

'Stone one's under the sink.'

'Right, Mrs Thwaite.'

'Netta, please lass.'

Tania smiled, glad she was here to help. 'Stay right there, Netta. I'll not be long.'

★ ★ ★

'We need to talk,' said Jake when the hot chocolate had been handed out to everyone seated round the large kitchen table.

'Aye, you only booked in for one night.' The farmer sounded harsh, but his eyes were twinkling.

'We don't intend to overstay our welcome,' Jake said stiffly.

'You'll not do that, lad.'

Jake frowned. 'But you've not room here for all of us?'

'Happen we have. And plenty of food too. Best get your stuff down from the bunkhouse now the snow's stopped again.'

Jake looked unconvinced. 'You've enough to worry about without us to think about too.'

'You'll stay right here. I'll not have your deaths on my conscience.'

'Deaths?' For a moment Tania thought she hadn't heard him correctly, but then she saw his lips twitch.

Lighter of heart now, she began to collect the mugs and carry them to the sink. Thank goodness they didn't have to move on just yet, or worse still return to the icy bunkhouse with no food or warmth.

She could see that the others were as relieved as she was. Only Jake seemed perturbed. Their eyes met and in them she saw a wary determination not to give in too easily.

'Gregor can do those when he comes down,' Jake said. 'I'll see what I can do to help Bill while you organise a trip to the bunkhouse for our gear, Tania, just in case we have to stay on.'

'Sure. But I'll just check on Netta, Mrs Thwaite, first shall I?'

'Netta now is it?' Bill said in approval. 'You tell her she's got to rest. I'd best get back now. We're nearly clear at the barn.'

Tania was down in minutes, having found the patient asleep. She ushered the girls and the two younger boys outside amid groans as they pulled on damp jackets and boots. The dog, Aussie, greeted them with rapture.

'Can he come too?' asked Max.

'Better not,' said Tania.

Now that the snow had stopped again visibility was improving and trudging along the path they had cleared earlier was easy.

'Where will we be tonight?' Wayne

asked as Tania locked the bunkhouse door behind them.

'Jake will make an announcement pretty soon I should think. OK?'

'I want to stay here.'

'In the bunkhouse?'

'At the farmhouse.'

'Me too,' said Max, his eyes shining. 'Can we, Tania? Can I see the ewes in the barn? Bill says they'll be having twins in April. How does he know?'

'My mum had twins,' said Collette, sliding along at Tania's side. 'They didn't survive, though.'

'Oh Collette, that's dreadful,' said Tania in sympathy.

'They weren't proper size babies. They'd hardly started to grow.' Collette's feet shot from under her and she landed with a thump on the ground. Unconcerned, she sprang up.

'Will the ewes' twins die?' asked Max.

'I shouldn't think so,' said Tania, hoping she was correct. 'Are you all right, Collette?'

The girl grinned at her, pulling her hat down further over her bushy hair. 'I'm always all right, me. Race you to the door, Max.'

With her longer legs Collette was back at the farmhouse first. She piled the laden rucksacks she was carrying against the wall and the others did too. Aussie shook the snow from his black and white body and stood guard over them.

Then, laughing, Collette grabbed a handful of snow and hit Max on the shoulder. Retaliating, he shouted in delight and soon all them were in a flurry of flying snowballs.

Ducking from the onslaught, Tania went into the warm kitchen, marvelling at Collette's resilience to all that she had had to contend with in her young life.

She peeled off her jacket and hung it over a chair as Jake came in. He removed his jacket too and steam rose from it into the warm air.

'I'll check on Netta,' she said.

'One minute, Tania, before Bill and his sons get back.' He looked full of resolution standing there with his feet apart and with his back to the Aga. From his flushed face it seemed that his bulky jersey was far too warm now that he had come in from the cold.

'You're not really thinking we can go further today?' she asked in sudden suspicion. 'Tell me it's not true.'

The earnest expression on his face didn't waver. 'I need your backing in this,' he said. 'Bill's tractor and snowplough will be in action soon clearing the track to the road and then we can check if it's possible.'

'But how can it be possible in blizzard conditions?'

He raised an eyebrow. 'Blizzard conditions? I think you're exaggerating, Tania. It's not even snowing now.'

'But it has been. It came down really hard in the night and could again. The sky looks full of it.'

'We're not giving up that easily.'

'But why not? How can it be

anything but dangerous when we've got to go over the top on really high ground and there's no shelter?'

'I shall be the judge of that.'

She glanced out of the window, wishing blizzard conditions still raged with thunder and lightning overhead. Thunderbolts would be helpful at this moment and the odd whirlwind churning up the snow into great sheets of impassable drifts so that there would be no doubt of the foolishness of even thinking they could manage it.

A lump of apprehension caught in her throat. With the phone out of order they couldn't even phone home to say that all was well. Dad would be concerned enough without their going on in these conditions unable to alert anyone of where they were.

'It's utter madness,' she said. 'Why does going on with the route mean so much to you, Jake?'

'You don't understand even now, do you?' he said, his voice bitter.

'I understand that the weather

conditions make it impossible.'

'Failure to complete the challenge is impossible. Psychologically impossible.'

'For the youngsters or yourself?'

He didn't answer and she looked at him for a long moment. Had she inadvertently hit on a truth he wouldn't acknowledge even to himself?

Loud thumping on the staircase alerted them to Gregor's appearance a moment later in the kitchen. His dark hair stood up in peaks and his face was flushed.

He looked a different boy from the scared one hovering in the hay in the barn.

'Better now?' said Jake. 'Raring to set off again on our travels?'

'What have you done with your wet clothes?' Tania demanded.

Gregor shrugged. 'Who cares? I'm off outside.'

Tania clenched her hands at her side to stop herself from leaping at him to confront him about that arrogant expression on his face.

'Everything revolves round you, doesn't it, Gregor?' she cried. 'Or that's what you like to think. You're a bully and a selfish skiver. It's about time you pulled your weight like the rest of us instead of causing mayhem wherever you go.'

With a surge of shame she listened to her ranting, but she couldn't stop now. She gave a great gasping breath. 'Instead of being a drag do something useful for once, can't you? Talk some sense into Jake.'

'What?'

'Make Jake see that we've got to stay here overnight, challenge or no challenge.'

Gregor stared at her. 'How'll I do that?'

'That's your problem. Work something out and do it. I'm about to check on Bill's wife. By the time I get down again I want it all sorted. Understand?'

With a furious glance at Jake's stunned face, Tania rushed out of the kitchen, her shoulders shaking.

A Change of Plan

Tania was still trembling as she reached the landing. For a few breathless moments she leaned on the banisters in an effort to calm down.

She had bawled Gregor out in front of Jake for doing no more than leaving his wet clothes on the bathroom floor. Typical teenage behaviour. She shuddered at the thought of facing Jake again when she went downstairs.

Deeply ashamed of her outburst, she took another deep breath and opened Netta's bedroom door.

Suddenly there was the roar of an engine overhead and Tania rushed to the window.

'The helicopter?' said Netta, raising herself on one elbow.

'I can see it now. It's low.'

'Checking that all's well.'

All at once the snow seemed to Tania

to sparkle more brightly. The men on board would have seen that Jake's group was safe here at Slough Fell Farm and could pass the information on to their families and guardians.

No-one need worry that they were caught out somewhere without shelter. She could just imagine the shock headlines in the paper if they had been stuck in the middle of nowhere.

Irresponsible group of youngsters rescued from the wild wastes. Leader, Jake Anderson, has much to answer for. Lessons will be learned.

Smiling at the thought, she gazed at the bleak world outside that was beautiful to her now. Lower down, the river was a silver ribbon and the stone walls on the hills on the other side were like thin dark wires on the white background. The helicopter circled round once more and then the engine sound faded as it disappeared over the far hill.

The silence was golden now she didn't feel they were so isolated. Netta, too, seemed to have a slight glow about her as she pulled her pink bed jacket on and smoothed her dark hair away from a face that didn't seem quite as drawn as yesterday.

She returned Tania's smile. 'Happier now, lass?'

'The kettle's hot downstairs,' Tania said. 'I'll bring something up for you.'

Netta lay back on her pillow. 'Aye, when it suits.'

'It's so lovely out there and so peaceful,' Tania said. 'I think we'd all like to stay on here at Slough Fell.'

Except one of us, she thought as she went to check on the state of the bathroom.

The steamy atmosphere still lingered, but there was no sign of Gregor's dumped clothes. A result here at least, she thought. Gregor might even have got Jake to see sense while she had been with Netta. But how likely was that? Dream on.

Gathering her courage she went downstairs. Jake, his back to her, was gazing out of the window. He was so still that she hesitated, fearful of his reaction when he realised she was there. Gregor shot Tania a look of triumph. Quietly she set about making a hot drink for Netta.

Then the back door crashed open and Max burst in amid a flurry of cold air, followed by Wayne.

'What's wrong, Max?' said Tania, rushing to her brother's side. 'Are you hurt? What's been happening?'

'It's nothing,' said Max, rubbing he cheek with his gloved hand. 'There's message from Bill. He needs help now getting some food supplies in from the freezer in the barn at the back.'

'Then see to it, can't you?' said Jake, spinning round. 'There are enough of you around doing nothing, aren't there?'

Max recoiled at the anger in Jake's voice. 'But he wants you and Tania to come, not us.'

Jake indicated with a nod of his head that the boys should join the others in the snow and all three went without argument. He turned to Tania. 'Come on, then.'

Outside, the bitter chill of the wind bit at her face as she trudged with Jake to the barn at the back of the house. The closed expression on his face was forbidding. She could see by the stiff line of his shoulders that his opinion of her was at an all time low. Well, that was all right. She expected nothing less. She didn't approve wholeheartedly of him either.

A massive freezer lived in this barn as well as another fridge and a washing machine. The floor had recently been swept clean and there was a faint scent of hay and corn about the place.

Bill had the lid of the freezer open and was reaching into its depths for some loaves of bread.

'I'll get these indoors now to defrost before I get off to the ewes,' he said, straightening. 'See what's here and take what you want. It'll need using up if the power's off for long. Aye, it'll do for a start and there are vegetables indoors.' He closed the lid. 'We won't waste the cold air while you decide what you want to use.'

'It's a feast,' said Tania, impressed.

'You'll make an evening meal for the lot of us?'

'We will that,' said Jake. 'And thanks.'

'Good lad. There's a bit of work for you later getting wood in for the fire in the holiday cottage out the back. It'll warm the place by tonight and suit you and the lads. The spare room at the house should do for the girls.'

Jake nodded.

'We've a couple of sledges over there. They need cleaning up a bit. Haven't been used for a good few years, but you can use them. I'll be off then.

'So that's that,' said Jake when he had gone.

Tania gazed at him in astonishment.

'What's wrong?' he asked.

She felt an awkward smile flicker on her lips and then die. 'So we're staying here tonight after all?'

'We'll need to get off at first light tomorrow to make up the lost time.'

'But we'll be safe here for now.'

'Safe yes, but behind schedule. We have to crack on, Tania. Our route is a circular one, planned to get us back on Wednesday to where we left the Land Rover. Two more nights. Once we're over the top it's a shorter distance, but we're on higher ground.'

'But we could get back quicker the way we came,' she pointed out.

'And fail to complete what we set out to do?'

'Please, Jake, I need to understand, truly understand why it means so desperately much to you that we do it this time when weather conditions are dead against us. No-one would think badly of us surely?'

'It's important that we don't think badly of ourselves. For their self esteem those four youngsters need to know they can battle against the elements and by not giving in achieve something worthwhile. That's what we can give them, Tania, don't you see, a belief in their own worth? They've had little enough of that in their young lives.'

'I can see that but . . . '

'And your brother? Isn't it good for him to do this thing too?'

'Well, yes, but not if it's dangerous.'

He looked at her searchingly. 'You think I would lead us in to danger just to boost my own ego?'

She was silent, considering. Jake was experienced. He was trusted by the guardians of the four in his care. But how much did they know of what was actually involved? He was brave and confident, but she had Max to think of. Jake knew that when she had agreed to come. It was fair, surely, for her to have some say in this?

'Jake . . . ' she began but then thought better of saying anything more. She should be thankful he had agreed to stay here tonight and not worry about the problems of the next day until it came.

'There's nothing more to be said on

the subject, Tania. Please understand that.'

She caught a flicker of something in his eyes and looked away, confused. All at once she wanted to console him as he stood there looking uncertain now about the decision that had been forced out of him. Surprised at her reaction, she stayed motionless, considering why this should be.

He opened the freezer lid and peered inside. 'Are you going to help me with these or not?' he said.

Silently they loaded a couple of handy boxes with packs of sausages, bacon and frozen peas. He seemed full of purpose suddenly and when he had snapped shut the lid again she stood back and gazed at him. He was taking this well for a man who had planned this trek for so long and which was likely to come to an end at Slough Fell if conditions didn't improve.

'I'm sorry it's worked out like this,' she said quietly.

He nodded. 'We'll cope.'

'I'm also sorry I shouted at Gregor.'

He nodded again and then gazed up at the roof of the barn. 'A fine building,' he said. 'Look at the way the beams converge in the centre.'

She looked up at them too, tilting her head back. The beams were obviously old and weathered. They looked strong and beautiful.

'I'm surprised Bill and his family haven't put the building to better use,' he said.

'You'd have some suggestions to make?'

'Are you doubting my ability?'

'Would I dare?'

'I think you would dare a lot more than that if you had to, Tania. Don't underestimate yourself.'

She looked at him questioningly. Did he intend that as a compliment? His good opinion of her was suddenly important.

'It would be an ideal place for groups such as ours to come for weeks at a time,' he said. 'Think of the surroundings, think of the outdoor activities even in the winter. The place could be in constant use, bringing in extra income for Bill and his family. Netta does bed and breakfast in the season, but this would be another more lucrative string to their bow.'

'You're serious about this, aren't you?' she said.

He shrugged. 'I'll get the boys help get this lot indoors,' he said.

Jake Relents

Snow began to fall again while they were eating their vegetable soup. Bill joined them at the house for a short time and then, when he had got togged up again in his outdoor clothes, his sons came in to eat too.

'Are they all right, those sheep in the barn?' asked Max. 'Are the lambs born yet?'

'Nay, lad,' said Neil, the eldest of Bill's sons, spreading a lavish amount of butter on his bread. 'Not till April or the back end of March maybe.'

'But we won't be here to see them.' Wayne looked hopeful. 'Not unless we're still snowed in.'

'Dad's off up to the tops with the dogs,' said Neil.

'A couple of ewes are missing,' said Andrew, the younger son.

122

'Will they be buried in the snow?' asked Max.

Neil pushed his chair back. 'He'll likely find them on the leeward side of a wall where the snowdrifts form. We'd best be off as well.'

'Can I come too?'

'No,' said Jake sharply.

Max looked disappointed. 'But I'd be kind to the sheep when they get dug out.'

'If they do,' said Gregor.

★ ★ ★

By the time they had all finished lunch and everything was cleared away, the afternoon was closing in and even the keenest of the snowballers were glad to huddle round the Aga in the kitchen.

Jake and Gregor went off to the wood store and carted loads of wood to the holiday cottage on the sledges they rescued from the barn.

While they were gone Tania organised the unrolling of the sleeping bags and the spreading of them out over the chairs to make sure they were aired.

She had just located the candles and matches that Netta told her were in the cupboard at the side of the fireplace when a shout of triumph went up. 'It's back on!'

In the sudden glare of the electric light all the faces looked pale. Everyone was grinning and slapping each other on the back.

Tania, checking on Netta, found her sitting up. She looked at her anxiously as she switched on the lamps on the dressing table and on the table beside the bed.

'I'm fine, lass,' Netta said, leaning back on her pillows.

'Are you quite sure?'

'Aye, I'm sure. And right glad I am to hear the sound of you all downstairs.'

'We're not disturbing you?'

'Not a bit.'

Suddenly the noises ceased as a door banged.

'TV's back on,' said Netta.

The three men were removing their boots in the kitchen when Tania got back downstairs. All three looked full of satisfaction at a job well done, their ruddy faces glowing in the warmth. From the Aga came the scent of jacket potatoes that she had placed in the oven earlier.

'We'll get the sausages and bacon on now you're back,' she said.

'That's grand, lass.'

Bill nodded his head in the direction of the other room where the noise of the television blared out. 'They're all set in there now?'

'They're fine,' she said, smiling at him. 'You found the ewes?'

'Aye, and brought them down,' said Bill.

'That's good.'

Jake looked at Tania. 'Like a quick check of the cottage while the rest of the food's cooking?' he asked.

'If there's time.'

'My team can see to things here. I'll rout them out.'

There was the crash of a door opening, excited shouts. Wayne rushed into the kitchen. 'Come quick, we're on the news!'

They followed him into the sitting room where Gregor had turned the volume on full blast. On the screen they saw an aerial view of a grey farmhouse and outbuildings sunk deep in a snowy landscape.

'Look!' Collete screeched. 'That's us.' She clung to Becky in delight.

Tania saw small figures, dark on the white background, and then the buildings becoming smaller as the helicopter swung round and away.

'That was us,' Max echoed in wonder. 'Tania, did you see?'

'We all did,' she said. 'Wonderful. I've never been on TV before.'

'But you're not there,' said Gregor.

'I was inside the house looking out,' Tania said firmly. 'That's good enough.'

'So it is,' said Jake smiling at her.

'Everyone'll see us,' said Wayne happily.

Jake smiled. 'Turn that sound down or we'll all be deafened if we're not already. Coming, Tania?'

She had her boots and jacket on in seconds and as they went out into the gloaming she took breaths of the cold air, glad to be here at Slough Fell with the prospect of a comfortable night before them. She felt for the camera in her pocket and pulled it out.

The pair of stone cottages, converted from some of the outbuildings, looked attractive in their plain simplicity. She held the camera to her eyes.

Jake paused and looked back. 'What are you doing?'

'Interesting subject in this light.'

He raised a questioning eyebrow. 'Interesting?'

'Not everyone would think so,' she said.

'But you do?' He sounded pleased.

'Look at the way the smoke from the chimney goes straight up,' she said. 'And the line of the roofs is so sharp against the grey sky. An ageless scene, don't you think? I want to capture it forever.'

Jake nodded. He hesitated for a moment as if he wanted to say something, but then seemed to think better of it. She wished he had told her something of what places like this meant to him.

He was an architect working for a firm who made a speciality of converting barns and outhouses such as these. He must have an opinion, surely, and she would like to hear it.

He opened the door of the first cottage, felt for the light switch and ushered her inside to a small room warmed and scented by the wood burning stove. A massive fire guard was in place and a large basket of logs stood at one side.

She took a breath of pleasure. 'You'll be comfortable here, Jake. But I think Max should be down at the house with us where I can check on him.'

'And why is that?'

She bit her lip, at a loss to answer.

He frowned. 'You baby that lad too much and it's not good for him. Have some sense, can't you, Tania? You're making a fool of him.'

She flushed. 'I'm trying to do my best for my brother, that's all,' she said.

'And I'm not?'

She opened her mouth to protest but then shut it again. Why had she come out with such a stupid remark if she didn't want to destroy the hint of friendliness between them that had been long in coming? A sudden awkwardness gripped her and for a second she couldn't breathe.

She smoothed her hand on the back of an easy chair. 'Of course you're doing your best for Max, Jake. I know that.'

A flicker of relief in his eyes came and went so suddenly she wasn't sure she had seen it.

'Two up and two down with the bathroom on the ground floor,' he said. 'Take a look upstairs, why don't you? Max stays here with us.'

She nodded and escaped up the narrow stairs. On the next floor there were two unmade single beds in each of the rooms, their mattresses covered with white sheets and ready for the sleeping bags the boys and Jake would bring with them at bedtime.

She could see that in the holiday season with duvets matching the flowered curtains at the windows these rooms would look comfortable and inviting.

'Lucky holidaymakers,' she said, downstairs again.

'Lucky us,' said Jake. He paused, a contented look about him as he gazed around him. 'In the eighteenth century this building and the one next to it were a cow mistle and granary.'

'Mistle?' she said. 'A lovely word.'

'Lovingly restored,' he said, a smile in his voice.

She giggled. 'Restored? Then shouldn't you be sleeping in cow stalls?'

His laugh was low and pleasant. 'You don't miss much, do you Tania?'

'Gregor won't try any nonsense again, will he?' she said.

Jake shook his head. 'We've sorted it out between us.'

Enough said. Tania took a quick look at the bathroom and was ready to go.

Reflections

The atmosphere in the farmhouse kitchen was a jolly one. Netta would be listening to the chatter, Tania thought, glad to feel part of things even though she was confined to bed upstairs. In a minute or two she would check on her again to make sure that all was well.

The lamp on the dresser had been lit even though with the overhead light no-one really thought it necessary. Talk was of the sledging they would do next day if they got up really early.

Jake, his face glowing in the warmth, made no mention of his hopes for moving on and Tania was content to sit back and enjoy the meal and company.

Afterwards when the clearing up had been done the girls settled in their bedroom upstairs while Jake accompanied the boys to the cottage. He then returned to check that all was well at the house. Tania heard the crunch of his boots outside the door and pulled it open to let him in.

'Everything all right here?' he said, stamping his feet on the doormat. 'Bill and his sons gone up?'

'Andrew's still out in the barn.'

He nodded. 'Keeping watch, I suppose. It's a hard life.'

He pulled back the curtain at the kitchen window and peered out. 'Those ominous clouds have cleared right away now,' he said. 'And just look at the moon.'

'It's so clear and beautiful.'

Tania stood beside him and gazed out at the moonlight sparkling on the snow. The shadow of the porch looked black on the white ground. The stars were so glittering she felt she could reach out a hand and touch them.

It was such a magical moment that in some incredible way Jake's spirit seemed to reach out to her in the beauty of it all. She hardly dared breathe in case the spell was broken.

They were silent in a companionable way that she wouldn't have thought possible a few hours ago. She wanted to understand in her heart what made Jake the man he was.

There were depths in him she needed to know for her own peace of mind. It had crept on her gradually, this longing to be at one with him, and she couldn't understand how this should be. She had seen him with his charges sometimes stern, sometimes kind but always with the feeling that he cared deeply for their welfare just as she did for her brother's.

'It's stunning,' she murmured. 'There's something about this place that gets to me.'

'Me too,' he said, his voice gruff.

She felt him look at her and turned to meet his gaze. Then, unnerved by his closeness, she moved away a little.

'Tania . . . '

'Max feels it too. He loves it here,' she said quickly.

Jake's eyes narrowed. 'Ah yes, your brother.'

An awkward silence hung between them now. The wonder faded into nothingness and the starlight outside in the winter sky dimmed.

He dropped the curtain into position. 'It's getting late. I'd better be off. Good night, Tania. Sleep well.'

'Good night, Jake,' she said.

He shut the outside door behind him with a determined thump and her heart felt sore as she watched from the window as he trudged across the moonlit yard, pulling his jacket round him against the cold.

★   ★   ★

That night Tania dreamt of Ivan. The image of him swimming across the River Arno to the Uffizi Gallery in Florence pursued by maddened ewes was so real that she awoke, shuddering.

She sat up in bed with her head resting on her bent knees, trying to make sense of something that wasn't sense at all.

In her dream the sky was breathtakingly blue, the water of the emerald river shimmering in the heat and the bodies of the sheep were purple.

And Ivan himself? She couldn't remember. He was a shadowy figure moving effortlessly through the water without a ripple on the calm surface.

The moonlight had faded now but in the gloom she could just make out Becky and Collette curled up on their bunks. No problem there, only with herself and the aftermath of her ridiculous dream.

At first Ivan had seemed to understand her need to be around for her young brother because of the traumatic time Max had been going through since Mum died.

But then Ivan had become assertive and had even suggested that Dad was selfish expecting her to pass up chance of a trip to Florence.

She wondered now why she hadn't

mentioned the Florence trip to Dad.

With a start she realised that her dream was truer than she had imagined and that Ivan was merely a shadowy figure in her life. She had been taken in at first by into thinking that her liking for his company would grow into something more permanent. But now she saw, quite clearly, how wrong she had been.

The man who now filled her thoughts was the one she had spent the last few days with, the man whose disapproval of her had seemed only too apparent.

But this evening things had been different between them until, by a few foolish words that had slipped out without her meaning to voice them, she had spoilt even that.

Shivering a little, she lay down again, but still sleep wouldn't come. The silence was oppressive. How many hours until dawn came and she could look outside at a world she knew was still heavily sheathed in white?

She felt for her torch beneath her pillow and shone it on her wristwatch, taking care to hide the light inside her sleeping bag. Three o'clock. Hours to go yet. Today Ivan would be flying home. Or was it yesterday? Friday, Saturday, Sunday. Today was Monday. No, Tuesday. He would have flown home yesterday.

In their situation here it was hard to imagine that life on lower ground was going on as usual with planes landing and taking off. This area, high in the Dales, had featured on the local TV news last night.

She had thought then what an unforgettable experience it was for the young people in their care. She was sure that Max would always remember their time here at Slough Fell Farm.

Jake, though, with his thoughts on completing the challenge, didn't see it that way. He had brightened considerably when the forecaster had promised a rise in temperature in the next day or two.

Further Drama

Jake, also waking in the early hours, lay for a while staring up into the invisible rafters. When he had returned to the cottage last night, cold and down-hearted, the welcome warmth from the wood burning stove had cheered him considerably.

Bill was right when he assured him that the heat from it was enough to take the chill off the bedrooms upstairs if the doors were left ajar and the stove kept in all night.

Maybe he should check that all was well.

The ashy smell from the dying embers greeted him as he crept down the narrow staircase. The faint glimmer from them was all the light he needed.

Carefully he moved the fireguard to one side so he could place a couple of small logs in place. The embers sizzled as a tiny exploratory flame licked the edge of one of them.

He sat back on his heels and watched as more flames came to life. As a boy he had loved staring deep into the fire at his grandparents' cottage on the edge of Oxley. He had seen in it palace rooms that changed into smaller ones as the burning woods shifted a little.

He had often wondered if his fascination with slight changes that made huge differences was the beginning of his interest in the study of architecture and his decision to pursue it as a career.

He had convinced his parents that he could support himself financially during the long training to become qualified. He had worked hard at university and in any free time he could find though this left little time for socialising.

He had been fortunate at the end of those years to obtain a position in the firm of architects in Leeds dealing in barn conversions.

One of his last part time jobs had

been helping at a centre specialising in the various problems of young people and he still worked there now on a voluntary basis.

Also working there was Sarah and for a time it seemed that their friendship might develop into something more lasting.

When it didn't work out she moved off to a more lucrative position as companion to someone who needed company on the sunshine cruises she craved.

Sarah had sent postcards from exotic places, obviously revelling in the life she had chosen. He discovered then that his interest in the underprivileged youngsters was as important to him as working to preserve the nature of the Dales.

The idea of involving some of his charges in this sponsored fell walk had come to him as a brilliant spark like the flames erupting in front of him now.

He leaned forward to place more logs on the flames, larger ones this time that would burn down into a bank of embers that would ensure warmth until morning.

★　★　★

Tania awoke to the sound of a phone ringing downstairs. There were other sounds too, a door opening and shutting, someone falling over an impediment left too near the outside door, the rattle of metal on stone.

She sat up and swung her legs out of her sleeping bag. Early as it was she needed to be up and doing too because Bill would be wanting to get outside to his ewes if Netta was feeling better now.

Downstairs, one of Bill's sons, Neil, was standing by the Aga in his outdoor clothes with a large mug of steaming liquid in his hand. She saw at once that someone had already breakfasted.

'Tea,' he said. 'Like some? Dad's taken some up to Mum. It's a degree or two warmer outside today.'

'How is she?'

'None too good.'

She felt a stab of fear. Mum would have been like that two months before her baby was due with no warning that things would go so disastrously wrong.

But this was a different case. Surely it was and Netta would be all right?

'The phone's back on?' she asked.

'Aye, these two hours since.' Neil raised the mug to his mouth and took a large gulp.

Her hand shook as she helped herself from the pot on the table. 'I'm here to help all I can, Neil. You'll tell me if there's anything special I can do for your mum?'

'Aye, I'll do that if need be. Dad'll be down in a minute. He'll not be wanting to find me here.'

He had gone by the time his father came clumping down the stairs.

'How's Netta?' Tania asked.

'A bad night, off and on. Sleeping now.' Bill glanced at his watch. 'She'll not want a fuss made, but she's none

143

too good, lass. I'll be back in half-an-hour or maybe less to see what we should do.'

She nodded, seeing from his slow deliberate movements and the deep lines on his forehead that he was desperately concerned about his wife. 'I'll check on her all the time,' she promised.

'You do that, lass.'

'Do you mind of I use your phone first? I'll be brief.'

'Aye, and the rest of you if you want.'

Then he too disappeared outside, a shaft of damp air rushing in as he opened and shut the door. She heard the dogs snuffle a welcome and one of them give short bark.

She went into the hall, picked up the telephone receiver and dialled Dad's number at home. It was early but he must have left for work already because there was no reply.

She stared at the receiver as if it was to blame but how stupid was that?

Quickly she left a message to say that

they were all right here at Slough Fell Farm and Max was having a great time in the snow.

Netta was still asleep, breathing deeply. Relieved for the moment Tania went downstairs again.

★　★　★

Jake was the first of their party to appear, closely followed by the others. They burst into the kitchen trying to keep their voices down but not altogether succeeding.

Something seemed to be affecting them with a strange sort of excitement. The worried atmosphere in the house most likely. To lighten it she passed on Neil's message to Jake expecting him to let the boys and girls use the phone too.

Instead he shook his head slightly and suggested they got their belongings tidied to allow time for sledging as soon as he gave the word.

In the warm kitchen the light reflected from the copper pots on the shelf and the scent of toasted bread-crumbs dribbling from the toaster was pleasant. Becky's face was rosy from the warmth of the Aga and Tania knew that Collette revelled in being cut off from the outside world.

Max ate silently, every now and again glancing at the outside door for the sound of Bill coming back and wondering probably if he could go out with him later and see the ewes in the barn.

She slipped away from the table to look in on Netta again and found her awake.

'Aye lass,' Netta murmured. 'I'm fine here keeping warm.'

From the look of her Tania wasn't too sure and as she rejoined the others she was relieved to hear the sound of scraping boots outside as Bill came in. A few minute later she heard him come downstairs again and use the phone in the hall.

She waited, cold with anxiety.

'The emergency services,' he said,

146

sticking his head round the kitchen door. 'They'll get here when they can. I'll get back up to her.'

'Will the helicopter come again to rescue her?' asked Collette with interest. 'Can we watch what happens?'

'Little ghoul,' said Jake, helping himself to more bread.

'Someone'll come,' said Gregor. 'They always do for people like that . . . ambulances screeching, helicopters zooming in and landing. You see it on TV all the time. Everybody making a fuss.'

'Helicopters couldn't land here,' said Max. 'They'd sink in the snow like the lost ewes.'

'Sheep hide by the walls,' Gregor retorted. 'You wouldn't catch a helicopter hiding by a wall.'

'Quiet, you two,' said Jake. 'There's a problem here. Treat it with respect.'

'No-one has respect for me,' said Gregor scowling.

'Don't give me that, Gregor,' said Tania. 'How many people manage a fell walk in these wintry conditions like the one we're doing? Isn't that something to be proud of? Tell me that before you start complaining.'

'Who's complaining? I'm just stating a fact.'

'A ridiculous one,' said Jake.

'Aussie would get a helicopter out of the snow,' said Max.

Sounds of the dogs barking had Gregor bounding up. 'What's going on?'

Tania's heart leapt. 'Sounds as if the paramedics have got through.'

'Outside, the lot of you,' Jake said. 'But see you don't get in the way. You can take the sledges over into the sloping field down below.'

Everyone shot up from the table and began getting jackets and boots on. They crowded outside and the sounds of their voices faded into the distance.

'Best out of the way,' said Jake.

Bill must have been keeping a look-out and was back downstairs as soon as the paramedics' vehicle had driven down the track to stop as near as it could get to the house.

'Aye, I'm right glad to see you,' Bill greeted them as they emerged carrying a bag and a folding stretcher.

'Snow's clear lower down,' one of the men said as they came into the kitchen. 'It's up here it's right bad. We were lucky to make it.'

Bill nodded and wiped the moisture from his forehead with the back of his hand. He gave Tania a slight nod before following the men upstairs.

'We'll be thinking about moving on when we've cleared this lot.' Jake said, piling dishes.

Hardly hearing what he said, Tania helped him stow the uneaten food in the fridge and clear the table. They worked in silence, listening for sounds that would indicate what was going on.

More footsteps sounded outside and with a sharp command to the dogs, Neil came in.

'They'll be down in a minute,' Jake said.

'Aye.' Neil slumped down in a chair at the table. 'It's a bad job.'

They seemed to Tania to be upstairs for ages, but it couldn't have been more than ten minutes before Bill came down again followed by the two men carefully manoeuvring the stretcher with Netta strapped to it.

Jake held the back door open and Tania just had time to smile at Netta as the stretcher was carried out to the waiting vehicle. Bill had a few quick words with his son and then he climbed in too and they were driven away.

Tania watched until the vehicle turn right at the top of the track and she could see it no more. She let out the breath she was holding and then took another deep one.

'It's really serious,' she said.

Neil wiped his hand across his forehead. 'Aye. It is that. I'll get out to the barn again now. Happen one of the ewe's has started early.'

The two dogs, Striker and Bob, got

150

up from the mat in the porch and followed him as he strode off, calling to them as he went.

With Netta was no longer upstairs the house felt empty as if the heart had gone out of it. As it had, Tania thought with a shiver as Jake closed the outside door behind them.

'That's that,' he said. 'How soon can you and the girls get packed up here?'

She looked at him in astonishment. 'You actually want us to go on today?'

'Of course we'll go on,' he said. 'There's been no more snow and the temperature is rising. I'll notify Neil and Andrew at once.'

'But Jake, we can't. Not when we can help out here. Netta . . . '

'She's in the best possible place being looked after,' he said. 'In the circumstances we can't overstay our welcome here.'

'The snow higher up won't have cleared, Jake.'

'We'll keep to the road if necessary for as long as we can and that will shorten the distance we have to go over the top.'

'But it'll be impassable up there. It will all look the same, the sky and the land merging.'

'We'll manage.'

'But how can we be sure of getting through to the next place? Anderwick, isn't it? It's high up, exposed. You said so yourself.'

'I've been on the phone. Their side of the high top isn't as bad as here and they've cleared the tracks down to the bunkhouse.'

'But we still have to get up there.'

The look he shot her was keen and she could see by the muscle moving near his mouth that he was aware of the difficulties but was determined to leave.

'No arguments, Tania,' he said, his voice grim. This is important.'

'We'll have to get some food packed then. Bill won't mind.' She rested both hands on the table and took several calming breaths in an effort to suppress her deep anxiety in leaving Slough Fell at this traumatic time.

Jake was making a big mistake. Concentrating on planning nourishment for them all was the best she could do to help for the moment.

She looked up. 'Bill said to take what we wanted from the freezer. I'll get a casserole going for him and his sons and put it in the oven for later. At least give me time to prepare that.'

Jake nodded. 'Don't be long about it, then.'

She pulled on her boots and outdoor clothes. If she got a casserole into the Aga now it would be ready for Bill and his sons by such time as they were ready to sit down and eat it.

A watery sun was struggling through a bank of cloud as she emerged into air that still felt cold. She stood still, breathing deeply.

She had always thought of herself as being intelligent enough to form her own opinions about what was the right course of action and what was the wrong thing to do. And this was definitely wrong.

Soon she would have to make an important decision and be strong enough to stick to it.

★　★　★

She was glad to see that Max was too busy helping haul one of the sledges over the wall into the snowy field to notice her as she crossed the yard.

The others too seemed unaware of the looming crisis now as they laughed and shouted to one another. She would keep it that way as long as she could before deciding exactly what she was going to do.

Aussie bounded at her with wagging tail as she went into the barn. He seemed to be laughing at her as he lunged playfully at her side.

'Hey, get away. I've got work to do.' She tried to push him off. 'You're a beautiful dog,' she told him. 'But far too loving for your own good. Go on, Aussie, *sit*!'

To her surprise he did, but not for long. The temptation to come close to her again was obviously too much.

'This is ridiculous, Aussie,' she said, looking for something to use as a lead. A piece of binder twine was hanging from a nail on the wall behind the freezer.

Tied up to a handy iron ring in the wall, he seemed content to sit and watch her as she filled her box with everything she needed. But no way could she carry that back to the house and cope with a boisterous dog on the end of a lead at the same time.

'You'll have to wait here for a few minutes,' she told him.

He accepted that, too, luckily. He was an amenable dog, she thought, very well behaved except in the way that mattered most to a hill farmer because he was no use with the sheep. He was so affectionate he'd probably love them to distraction.

Collete, Becky and the boys had finished in the yard and were scrambling over the wall into the snow.

'I've left Aussie tied up in the barn,' she called. 'Can you fetch him, Gregor, while I get this lot indoors?'

Immediately she knew her mistake. 'No Gregor, get this box indoors while I get him,' she cried.

The look he gave her was scornful. 'Think I'm scared of a dog?'

'I'll go,' said Max. 'I'm not afraid.'

For a charged moment Gregor stared at the younger boy. Then, in sudden fury, he lashed out at him. Max, taken off guard, let out a cry as he landed on the ground. He sprang up at once, red-faced.

'Stay here the lot of you,' Gregor snarled as he strutted off round the corner of the house.

Tania dropped the box and rushed to her brother. She felt her feet slide from under her and she would have fallen if Collette hadn't grabbed hold of her. Becky and Wayne stood transfixed.

Too late now to stop Gregor reaching the barn. With a spurt of energy Tania rushed after him through the wide-open door, blinking in the gloom.

There was no boy here and no Aussie either.

'What's up?' said Jake from behind her.

She swung round, her face aflame. 'Aussie's gone. I tied him up here. Gregor went to fetch him.'

'*Gregor* did?'

'I sent him. I forgot he's afraid of dogs. And now he's gone.'

Jake's lips tightened. 'And no wonder. He witnessed his uncle's dog attack and injure his baby brother badly when he was a toddler himself. How do you expect him to react to dogs after that?'

Tania's hand flew to her mouth. She felt faint.

'So what happened?'

'Gregor knocked Max flying.'

'And?'

She shook her head, shocked at what he had told her. 'I didn't wait to find out. I went after Gregor.'

She felt Jake's gaze like a laser beam.

'Leave this with me.'

The tone of his voice was enough to send shivers down her spine. Numbly, she watched him stride off towards the cottage, slipping a little once or twice and then regaining his balance.

She dare not imagine what Gregor would do now or where he would go. And what of poor Aussie whose fault none of this was?

A Welcome Call

The phone rang and Tania rushed through to the hall to answer it.

'Slough Fell Farm,' she said breathlessly.

'Bill Thwaite here.'

'Oh Bill, how's Netta?'

'I'm to stay with her overnight. They'll see how she is in the morning. They say the babe'll be fine. The lads?'

'Still out in the barn. A bit of a problem down there with a couple of the ewes, I think.' She heard his sharp intake of breath but knew she couldn't keep this from him even though he didn't need it at a time like this.

'Aye. I'll be needing to phone every half hour or so to check,' he said. 'You'll tell them what's happening here, lass?'

'I'll get a message out to them,' she promised. 'And someone will be here indoors all the time to take messages.'

'That's grand.'

'Give Netta our love.'

'I will that.'

She replaced the receiver and stood leaning against the wall, weak with relief that Netta was safe in hospital and that the baby would be all right. But what about Netta herself? Bill was staying there tonight to be with her, but did that mean that there were serious problems? The phone rang again. She reached for the receiver but took a moment to regain her breath.

'So how's it going out there in the snowy wilderness? I was worried sick when I saw it on TV.'

'Annie?'

'That's me. Big and beautiful and home from York because the main speaker's in hospital and the course is cancelled. Bad luck or what? Phoning to report.'

Tania gave a strangled laugh. 'Oh Annie, I'm so glad to hear your voice, but I can't talk now. We've to keep the line clear.'

'For emergencies? So it's really bad there? Are you still snowed in?'

'Yes. No.'

'Make up your mind.'

'How did you know we were here?'

'From your dad, of course. I'll come at once.'

'No, don't, Annie. You might have difficulty getting through. We're perfectly safe here for the moment, but the road up from below could be a problem and I'd worry you'd get stuck. And we're all fine and the farmer and his two sons. Their mum's in hospital. We're making ourselves useful.'

'Even Cousin Jake? Don't tell me he's not champing at the bit eager to go off into the vast unknown.'

Tania took a deep breath. 'Get off the line, Annie, please.'

'So there *is* something wrong?'

'I'll phone later. Promise.'

There was a deep laugh on the other end before Tania heard the receiver being put down with more of a thump than was necessary.

She was surprised at how uplifted she felt. She returned to the kitchen forgetting for the moment that Gregor was missing and she was to blame. But then the worry of it came rushing back. Gregor hadn't gone far last time he'd taken himself off.

Maybe it was the same now. But how many more times was it going to happen, causing them all worry, Jake especially? He didn't deserve this.

A swift vision of his hurt expression when she had voiced her fears about leaving here shot in to her mind. He was a good man, intent on doing the best for the young people in his care and being let down by some of those that should be doing all they could to make things work.

But in her way she was doing that. She had nothing to feel guilty about, apart from being insensitive to Gregor's fears. And that, of course, was bad enough.

Collete and the boys had collected the scattered packets of frozen lamb by now, repacked them in the box and brought it indoors.

They were good kids. Tania was glad to see that Max seemed none the worse for Gregor's attack and anxious to get out to the sledging again while they had the chance.

'What's it all this for?' Collette asked.

'For the meal tonight, for those still here.'

'Still here?' Collete echoed in dismay. 'Why wouldn't we be here?'

Tania hesitated. She was almost certain that Jake's plans were to move on, but the announcement might be better coming from him. 'It's for Bill's sons mainly,' she said.

'Not for us?'

'They'll be specially hungry they've working so hard, but I'll make enough for us too. Want to give me a hand?'

'I will,' said Wayne. 'I like cooking.'

Collette and the others had already sidled to the door eager to escape.

Wayne was surprisingly helpful once she had defrosted the meat in the microwave. He carried the pieces to the floured board on the table and carefully coated them all over.

'We need a big frying pan and some olive oil so we can brown them before putting them in the casserole dish,' he informed her with importance.

'So you know what to do?'

He nodded. 'Trust me.'

They peeled the potatoes, carrots and onions between them and Wayne found a tin opener so that she could open three tins of Scotch broth to add with added water to the meat and vegetables.

'Don't forget the pepper and salt,' said Wayne.

At last it was ready to be placed in the Aga to cook slowly for hours. That done Tania turned her attention to washing up the utensils they had used.

'So where did you learn to cook, Wayne?' she asked.

He shrugged. 'My aunty and my grandad mostly until they died. Mum, too, when she was there. I like cooking, you see. I might decide to do a course at college one day. And then I'll be a real chef in a real restaurant.'

He sounded so grown up as he told her his plans for the future that Tania's heart was touched.

'And you're interested in bird watching too, Wayne? Was that because of your grandad?'

'Oh no,' he said. 'That was Jake.'

'Jake?'

'We go out at weekends about once a month, a crowd of us. He's going to give me a pair of binoculars for my birthday.'

What a paradox the man was, she thought, objecting to the lad getting his bird book out of his rucksack because it would hold them up on the walk for a few seconds and yet fostering a love of birds by giving him a generous gift.

'Failure's Not an Option'

To discover Gregor huddled in one of the armchairs in the cottage was a great relief to Jake although he hadn't thought the lad would have gone far.

A farm with working dogs was the worst place for Gregor, but so far he had seemed to be coping. With Striker and Bob at least. But the exuberant dog, Aussie, was a different matter.

He should have been more vigilant and made sure that one was kept right away from him at all times. It was his own failure that had caused this problem now.

The boy raised his head as he went in. 'What are you doing here?'

'Same as you. Come for a warm-up.'

'Don't believe it.'

Saying nothing, Jake picked up his pad and biro from the window seat and sat down. He didn't want the boy to think he was checking up on him. Once more his acting ability, such as it was, must come into operation.

'Has it occurred to you that there's a lot of wasted space here?' he said, looking up at the ceiling that was surprisingly high for such a small room. 'The two bedrooms have high ceilings too.'

'What of it?'

'This was once an outbuilding until it was converted into two holiday cottages. It's a pity they didn't put in an extra floor.'

'What would they want to that for?'

'Extra accommodation?'

Jake got up and prowled around, examining the door frame, tapping the wall above and then doing a rough measurement with his hand of the depth of the window sill. He tried to look completely immersed in what he was doing, but he was well aware of the troubled boy watching him.

He could see that Gregor looked interested.

'Mmm,' he said, hoping that he appeared deep in thought.

Gregor sat up straight. 'You mean that if you had the chance you'd make the place bigger so they could make more money?'

'Something like that.'

'But suppose they don't need more money?'

'I think they do.'

'With that big house and all these buildings and the fields and everything?' Gregor's voice was full of scorn.

'They could have a run of bad luck at any time if they get a bad season.'

'Is that what they're worried about now then, Andrew and Neil?'

'Partly, I suppose, but it's mainly the animals in their care.'

'But they're only sheep.'

'Animals mean a lot to their owners, Gregor.'

'More than people?'

'People don't own other people, Gregor.'

The boy was silent for a long

moment and Jake concentrated taking measurements for no reason at all.

'It would be easier to build on then as there's plenty of space outside,' Gregor said at last.

Jake nodded as he came and sat down again. 'Not as simple as that, I'm afraid, Gregor. Nothing ever is, especially in a national park.'

'Why's that?'

When Jake had finished explaining that planning laws were strict because of preserving the nature of the Dales he was surprised to find that Gregor's eyes weren't glazed with boredom.

'Years ago farm buildings were built from local materials and fit in well with the landscape,' he went on. 'They often have sandstone flags or slates for roofs.'

'And you'd have to use the same things for new bits added on?' Gregor was showing a definite interest now.

'Hideously expensive if they did. But new materials can be used if they fit in with the old. The best thing to do would be to discuss it with the planning officer and be prepared to take his advice.'

'So you'll do that then?'

Jake smiled. 'I don't own the place, Gregor. I only wish I did.'

'But if you did you'd want to enlarge it?'

'I'd think about enlarging it to sleep at least ten people. Ah well, dream on. I'd better get back and see what's what. Coming?'

For answer Gregor got up and crossed to the window. He stood with hunched shoulders appearing to be absorbed in the stonework surrounding the glass. But Jake had known him too long to be fooled.

It was fear of that wretched dog that had sent the boy to hide here and he could well understand that.

He moved to the door. 'Get your stuff packed, Gregor,' he said. 'I'll not be long rounding the others up.'

'Then what?' Greg asked, his voice suspicious.

'Do you fancy going on to the next place?'

Gregor's eyes brightened. 'Today?'

'Why not? Max is all right. We all are. Wait here and I'll be back.'

He closed the door behind him with a confident click.

★ ★ ★

Tania heard the back door open as she came down to the kitchen after checking the bedrooms for tidiness. Wayne, his job done, had gone to join the others outside. This was it, she thought, with a flicker of apprehension.

She would know now whether or not her careless words had caused more trouble for them all.

'Gregor?' she asked, her throat dry as Jake came in with a basket of logs.

'At the cottage.'

'Aussie?'

He shrugged. 'Who knows?'

'So Gregor's safe?' Relief flooded through her. She wouldn't worry about the dog any more. Aussie could take care of himself.

He nodded. 'How are things here?'

'Bill phoned. He's staying at the hospital overnight and wants someone to tell his sons.'

'I'll get on to that now. I've got to see them anyway to settle up in their father's absence.' He dumped the basket of logs near the door. 'I've brought these in case they're needed in the house. I'm letting the fire die down in the cottage now we're leaving.'

'So we're going?'

'I'll phone the next place and warn them to expect us in a few hours. We should make it tonight if we move fast.'

'And if we don't?'

'Failure's not an option.'

Turning her back on him, she began to unload the contents of the tray she had brought downstairs. Then she turned both taps on full and squirted a large amount of washing up liquid into the washing up bowl, not caring that froth reared up at her.

'But why, Jake?' she said. 'There's no need to go on. Gregor can keep right away from the dogs surely?'

'You know that's not the only point. We have to complete the challenge to give them that sense of achievement they need.'

She slashed the bubbles from her jersey. 'But why, why, why?'

He looked at her searchingly. 'You ask that?'

She took a deep breath and thrust a mug and empty soup bowl into the hot water and swirled them round.

'I believe that this is challenge enough for them here because they're doing something useful and know they're appreciated for it.'

'But that's not enough.'

'Aren't those youngsters more important than theories?'

'You think I regard Gregor and the others as theories?'

She turned to face him with the dripping dishcloth in her hand. 'Have you asked them what they want, Jake, let them in on the decision making too? No, you have not. And why not?'

'Ultimately this must be my decision.'

'You believe that battling on will be the best for them in the long run and because it's your belief it must be right.'

'Put that cloth down,' he said. 'I don't fancy it full in my face.'

She gave a frustrated snort as she threw the dishcloth into the bowl. 'What sort of monster are you to think like that?'

His face whitened. 'You believe that of me?'

'Didn't you take in what Neil said? One of the ewes is in trouble. Others might be too. Neil and his brother could be out there help them.

'Who's going to man the phone, cook hot meals and keep things running here as Netta would if she wasn't in hospital?'

'So I've got a mutiny on my hands?'

She stood up straight and looked him in the eye. 'We have to stay here for the next day or two whether we like it or not for the sake of Netta and the Thwaite family.'

'Even though it means failure in what we set out to do?'

'Even that.' She saw the hurt in his eyes and took a long deep breath for control. 'You're wrong, Jake,' she said more gently. 'The sense of achievement those kids have in knowing they're being useful here isn't so much different from the sense of achievement in completing the walk.'

'I think it is.'

'I disagree and because of that I've thought long and hard about my decision not to move on from here as long as we can make ourselves useful at Slough Fell.'

A long silence hung heavily between them.

'Gregor's deep fear means there's no sense of achievement here for him,' Jake said at last 'He'll bear the shame of that for the rest of his life. I set out to help him and now. I've failed in that too.'

'Gregor can keep away from the dogs, no problem,' she said. Instinctively she took a step towards Jake but he turned away from her.

'I'll take the logs back to the cottage,' he said.

She watched him go and stood staring at the closed door until the twist of pain round her heart faded into a dull ache.

She knew that whatever happened now Jake would always blame her for the decision that had been forced out of him.

An Unexpected Guest

The sounds of activity outside ceased suddenly. Tania, surprised, opened the door and looked out into an empty yard. She hoped they hadn't gone off down to the barn egged on by Max who desperately wanted to see for himself what was going on with the ewes that were causing Neil and Andrew so much concern.

But no, the distant voices were coming from the other direction which meant that the two boys and Collette and Becky had gone off elsewhere to discover new delights connected with the snow.

They at least were content to remain here, feeling part of the place whether they were aware of it or not because their being here benefitted other people. She wished Jake felt the same.

Satisfied, she turned to go inside

again and then heard the engine of a car grinding its way up the hill from below and taking ages to reach the place where the farm track turned off to lead steeply down to the farmhouse.

Now the vehicle gained speed because of the work Bill's sons had done in clearing and gritting.

Who could this be? She grabbed her jacket from the hook inside the door and went to investigate. From the way Annie had slammed down the phone, laughing, she wouldn't have put it past her to set off for Slough Fell Farm on impulse. But the approaching car wasn't her friend's Corsa so whose was it?

The man at the wheel of the four-by-four pulled up a short distance away from her. A black and white dog, leapt out as soon as the door opened.

'Aussie,' she cried, rushing forward to greet him.

The man with him caught hold of the dangling binder twine and yanked him back. 'I was expecting as warm a welcome for myself,' he said.

She gave a gulp of astonishment. 'Ivan! What are you doing here?'

'Apart from rescuing stray dogs, you mean? It's good to see you, Tania.'

'I can't believe this. Why have you come?'

'Aren't you pleased to see me?'

'But where did you find Aussie?'

'Wretched dog slobbering all over me! I don't know why I bothered to stop down the road by the bridge over the river. I opened the door and in he got. I should have kicked him straight out and be done with it. I was lucky to get going again, I can tell you. The road down there's a skating rink.'

Relieved to see the dog again, Tania fell down at Aussie's side and hugged him. He squirmed in ecstasy licking her face and struggling to get into her lap.

'Max will be pleased,' she said, standing up again and taking the binder twine lead from Ivan. 'Thanks for bringing him back, Ivan. It was good of you.'

'And that's all you can say?'

'I'm really surprised, that's all.'

'I only got back home last night and heard the news.'

'About us being snowed in?'

'I couldn't believe what I was hearing about you still being all the way up here in this weather when your friend told me where you were. I was astonished. I can tell you.' He gave an exaggerated shiver. 'So I assumed you'd be frozen to death in some godforsaken place and needed rescuing.'

'And you've come all this way just to check?'

The expression in his eyes softened. 'I've been worried about you, Tania. I needed to see for myself that you were safe.'

She gave a tremulous laugh, pleased at his concern, but distressed at the same time that his journey was unnecessary. 'We're fine,' she said. 'Annie should have told you. We're staying here at this comfortable farmhouse. It couldn't be better. But it was good of you, Ivan, to take the trouble to check.'

To her horror her lips trembled. She pressed her hand against her mouth.

He looked at her closely. 'It's easy to see that something's wrong.'

She shook her head, ashamed of her weakness. 'No, really.'

All sounds of Collette, Becky and the boys had vanished now and she suspected they had taken cover, suspicious of a stranger who turned up unannounced. She untied Aussie and he bounded off to join them.

'Best come into the house,' she said. 'Coffee?'

'I thought you'd never ask.'

Indoors, she removed her boots and shrugged herself out of her jacket. Ivan took off his jacket too and then stepped towards her and took her in his arms.

Taken by surprise, Tania went limp for a moment and then pulled away before he had a chance to kiss her. 'No, no, Ivan, please . . . '

'I've come to take you home, away

out of here,' he said. 'And your brother too, of course. I care about your safety, Tania, and about you too.'

'But we're fine.'

'I can't believe that.' He hooked a chair out from the table and sat down. 'Now come on, my love, tell it as it really is and I'll understand, I promise. I missed you in Florence more than I could have imagined.'

With her back to him Tania busied herself with the kettle. When it boiled she made coffee and sat down opposite him. 'I can't come home with you, Ivan,' she said.

'But why not?' He sounded so demanding she was startled.

'I'm committed to the job I'm doing here. I want to stay and do what I can while I'm needed.' She bit her lip, aware that she sounded pious and prissy.

'Now come, on Tania . . . '

'Did you have a good time in Florence?' she said in an effort to lighten the atmosphere.

He sighed. 'So-so.'

'Was the Uffizi Gallery as wonderful as you expected?'

He shrugged off her mention of the gallery as if it hadn't existed for him. And perhaps it hadn't if what he'd shown about his renewed feelings for her were uppermost. Concerned, she struggled to act calmly and took a sip of hot coffee that slithered down her throat like molten lead.

He picked up a teaspoon and looked at it. 'Nothing was good without you at my side, Tania. I knew it wouldn't be, of course. I was desperately hurt that you refused to come with me.'

They had been through this so often and she couldn't take any more now. She stood up, carried her coffee to the sink and poured it away.

He looked at her in alarm. 'What are you doing?'

'I thought I'd made my feelings quite plain the last time we met,' she said quietly. 'They haven't changed, Ivan. I'm touched that you were concerned about me, but I think you should go now that you know that all is well with us here.'

He gazed at her in silence for a long moment. She tried to look away, but there was an intensity about him that alarmed her.

He stood up, scraping his chair back. 'I can see you're not yourself, my love,' he said, obviously making an effort to soften his voice. 'I'm aware that you've had a worrying few days not knowing how to escape, but it's ending now. I can have you safe and sound at home in no time. You'll feel better then. What do you say?'

She held herself in with difficulty. 'I've already told you and I'm sorry, Ivan.' She felt near to tears.

He gazed at her, smiling slightly. 'But not to worry,' he said. 'If you'd like another night here I can understand. I'll come back tomorrow, no problem. There's a place back down the road where I can book in. The woman said she'll keep a room for me. Gillerthwaite's the name of the place. Not far in a car.'

'Miss Crabbe?' Tania had a swift vision of the kind old lady in the dimness of her shop and the basket of ginger and white kittens in the corner. It seemed weeks ago that they were there.

'That's the one. Until tomorrow then.'

'No, Ivan, please . . . '

He went and, filled with deep weariness Tania sank down at the table and stared at his untouched coffee.

Challenging Gregor

The meal that evening was a sombre one in spite of the meaty smells from the casserole in the kitchen lit as usual by lamplight with the warmth from the Aga making their faces glow.

'By, it's cold out there!' said Andrew, throwing open the door after a lot of noisy stamping of feet on the mat outside. He shut the door quickly, shrugging off his bulky jacket and moving to the Aga to warm his frozen hands.

'More snow?' Max asked eagerly.

'No lad. Temperature's well below zero. Too cold for snow.'

'But more snow might come,' said Wayne.

'Eat your food,' Jake said sharply.

Becky gave him a fearful look and slid down a little in her chair.

Tania dished out a steaming plateful

and carried it across to the table for Andrew. 'Will Neil be in soon?'

'Aye, as soon as I get back down there.' Andrew looked troubled as he picked up his knife and fork. 'There's another long night ahead of us for sure. I'll need to get back out there fair smartish.'

'I'll fill another flask,' said Tania.

Jake looked up. 'More problems?'

'Seems like it. We could do with Dad.'

Jake nodded, pushed his chair back from the table and stood up. 'Take your time, Andrew. Don't get indigestion. I'll get down there for a while so you get the chance for a bit of a rest. You need it.'

He thrust his arms into his jacket and pulled on his boots. As soon as Tania had the flask ready he was off. Andrew cleared his plate and stood up, refusing the apple crumble Tania put on the table. 'That was grand, lass, but I must get back.'

She nodded and didn't try to

dissuade him. He and his brother knew what they were about and Neil needed a meal too.

Bill's elder son seemed to stumble as he came in and sat down at the table. His face was ashen pale and there were dark shadows beneath his eyes. The strain was obviously getting to him.

He looked up, nodded his thanks as she placed his meal in front of him, and then sat for a moment, looking down at it.

'Don't let it get cold,' Collette said.

Tania could see the effort it was for him to pick up his knife and fork. Responsibility lay heavily on him and was enough to deaden any appetite, especially with the added worry about his mother.

The others had finished now and were happy to escape to the TV in the other room. Only Gregor hung back.

Neil got to his feet. 'I'll be on my way,' he said, his voice slurred.

'He's exhausted,' Gregor said when he had gone. He eyed the remains of the apple crumble.

Tania pushed it across to him and sighed. 'I'm afraid so, Gregor. I wish there was something you could do to help out like taking another flask down there later in case they need it.'

'Me? You're kidding!'

'Why should I be kidding? You see how it is with the pair of them. Or you could help me wash up.'

Gregor gave a scornful look at the table. 'No way.' He got up put on his outdoor things and peeped cautiously outside. 'The dogs aren't there.'

He was gone before she could remonstrate, but what was the use anyway? If he was determined to set off on his own again she couldn't physically stop him without help. But why would he in this weather? All the same she had an anxious few minutes before he came back again.

'Jake said you're to come,' he said breathlessly. 'He needs your help.'

'He does?' She rushed to do as he said, Gregor following.

Tania felt the icy ground slip away from her once or twice as she followed.

Down near the barn where the ewes were housed they found Neil on the ground with Jake kneeling beside him.

'Has he hurt himself?'

By now Neil was in a sitting position, holding his shoulder and muttering that the ground was lethal. Between them they helped him to his feet.

'Shaken that's all, I think,' Jake muttered. 'I'll get him back to the house with Gregor's help.'

'What about Andrew . . . ?'

'Take over there, will you, Tania? Do your best.'

'Right.'

'I'll be back as soon as I can.'

Close Comfort

Tania pushed open the barn door and slid inside. To her relief nothing seemed to be happening, no heaving of frantic sheep or pools of blood, just the smell of damp straw and the sounds of sheep stirring a little and muted bleats from the early arrivals snuggling into the warmth of their mother.

Andrew looked up from the bale of straw he was seated on. His expression didn't change when he saw her though he must have wondered what she was doing here.

'All quiet?' she said.

'Aye. For the moment. One needs watching. Signs of a difficult time ahead of her, right enough.'

'Jake'll be back in a minute,' she said. 'He's taking your brother back to the house. Neil had a fall. Jake thinks he's just shaken, but wants to be sure though Neil looked dreadful. Jake will take over here tonight instead of him.'

'Jake's a good lad.'

Tania sat down on an adjoining bale. She could see now that the ewe who'd recently given birth to twins was in a pen of her own.

She wondered where the dogs were and looked round expecting to see them curled up fast asleep in a corner. But how likely was that? Their nearness would probably worry the expectant ewes out of their wits.

'So where are Striker and Bob?' she asked.

Andrew nodded at the door. 'There's a small room down beyond full of straw. They like it there, Aussie too. Warm, you see, on a cold night and right handy if they're needed.'

She nodded, knowing how pleased Max would be to know that Aussie was comfortable and warm.

Andrew got up to take a look at the ewe that had problems and beckoned to Tania. She was quickly at his side.

'Get some more water ready from the tap in the corner. The bucket's there.'

She heaved it back, full, and placed it where it would be safe from being knocked over. 'Anything else?'

'I'll likely need you to hold her steady in a bit. Pass those towels.'

She passed them across and as he did so the barn door opened and Jake came in on a blast of cold air. He came straight to her and caught her in his arms.

'All right?' he said.

'Oh Jake,' she murmured, so relieved to see him that she leant against him because it seemed the natural thing to do. She felt his strength flow into her.

He held her tightly for a moment and then released her. 'I'll take over here now and stay all night if needed. You can cope with everything else?'

'Of course.'

'Good girl.' The confidence in his voice was uplifting.

★   ★   ★

Back at the house she found Gregor in the kitchen.

'What's going on now?' he demanded.

'Jake's staying there in the barn until the morning. The dogs are shut up in a room of their own.'

'So everything's OK?'

She sank down at the table. 'If you say so.'

'I never took a flask down.'

She stared at the spare one on the draining board. 'It might be better to fill it with hot soup. There's a lot left in the casserole dish. That would do.'

For the first time she realised that there were no dirty dishes piled high by the sink and the table had been cleared. 'Did you do this, Gregor?'

'Someone had to, didn't they?'

She got up. 'I'll fill that flask.'

When he had gone again she stood leaning against the Aga waiting for him to come back and thinking of those few moments in Jake's arms when she had felt warm and safe. He had praised her, too, and that was sweet. She would hold on to that in the time ahead.

After a minute or two she let out a lingering breath to bring herself back to the present problems. She was in charge of the house for the night and the young people in it. There were things to do.

She and the girls would stay here of course, but the boys? Gregor in the cottage with Max and Wayne? That thought was worrying and not only because of the wood burning stove. That would be safe enough with its fireguard or they could let it go out. But no, not in these falling temperatures. And she couldn't keep going from one building to the other checking that all was well.

There was nothing for it but to move the boys here.

Taking Care of Business

Next morning Tania woke with a start and lay listening for a while to the silence outside. Presumably Jake and Andrew had spent all night in the barn because she hadn't been aware of any disturbance in the small hours.

It was early yet, hardly light, and there was no sound from the other bedrooms here in the house.

The initial objection last night from Gregor to moving themselves over here was immediately squashed by an anxious-looking Wayne. But none of the boys had really minded carting their belongings across to the house in the moonlight.

With armfuls of bedding they slithered about on the path that had iced up since they had cleared it and made a great deal of noise about it.

While they were doing that, Tania had moved out of her room and into the one occupied by Becky and Collette. She would be comfortable enough there on the floor.

This meant that there was room for Max and Wayne to sleep in her room. Gregor was content to use the long sofa in the sitting room. She suspected that having the TV in there had something to do with it.

Now she raised herself on both elbows, checked that the girls were still asleep, and then crawled out of her sleeping bag. Grabbing her clothes, she crept out onto the landing and into the bathroom to dress in there.

Downstairs, she filled the kettle and put it on the Aga ready for whoever appeared first. A few moments later Andrew came into the kitchen from the hall, rubbing his eyes and yawning.

She looked at him in surprise.

'Aye, it's me,' he said.

'I didn't hear you come in. Where's Jake?'

'I'm to relieve him at seven and it's that now.'

'He's been there all night?'

'Aye. Things quietened down after a while. He'd fetch me if need be. He'll be ready for his bed now.'

Tania looked at the kettle, willing it to boil. 'Like a cup of tea before you go, something to eat?'

The tea was made by the time Jake came. If she hadn't known that he'd been out in the barn all night she might have thought he'd merely been outside for a quick look around.

He came in breezily enough, proud no doubt of his responsibility to those sheep and the help he was able to give Neil and Andrew. She hoped it made up to him a little for his failure, as he saw it, to the young people with whom he had set out from home a few days ago with such high hopes.

She thought she saw a glimmer of something in his eyes as he saw her, but then it was gone again and weariness seemed to fill him suddenly.

'Here, sit down and drink this,' she said, pushing a mug of steaming tea across the table towards him.

He sat for a moment with his hands wrapped round it and his head bent. A rush of sympathy engulfed her and for a moment she wondered how all this was going to end. The snow was their enemy and it seemed impossible that it would ever go.

'Still as cold outside?' she asked.

He nodded. 'Bitter.' He picked up the mug and took a sip from it and then put it down again.

'Andrew said you were on your own.'

'He needed some rest after all the hours he's put in. There was nothing else for it. He couldn't go on as he was. He said that Neil had a disturbed night. No surprise there. I'll check on him before I go over to the cottage. I need to get my head down.'

Tania poured tea for herself and sat down. She hadn't thought to ask Andrew about his brother until it was too late and he had gone striding off to the barn to relieve Jake.

Jake looked up. 'The boys . . . ?'

'I got them over here. It seemed best. I'll see they don't disturb you.'

He gave a massive yawn, glanced at his watch and then downed the rest of his tea.

* * *

'I need someone to go up and check on Neil,' Tania said as Gregor came into the kitchen rubbing his eyes.

'Down in the barn?' he said, bemused.

'Wake up, Gregor. Neil's in bed upstairs. I bet you have a good night stretched out on that sofa. Or were you catching up on the TV?'

He scowled. 'What have I got to do?'

'I'll have your breakfast ready when you get down again. Just take a look at him and see if he's awake. That sort of thing.'

'What's for breakfast?' Gregor asked suspiciously.

'Will a bacon butty do you?'

He was gone at once. She heard a

door open upstairs, voices, a clumping sound across the landing. Then Gregor was back.

'His shoulder hurts,' he said. 'And his ankle. He had to hop across the bathroom. He looks all right, though.'

'That's what a night's sleep in a bed does for you,' said Tania, busy with setting a tray. 'You'd better take this up to him. Then we'll see what can be done.'

She wondered at her calmness in the face of this new potential problem, but for the moment she must cope with breakfast for them all.

During the clearing up afterwards the phone rang.

'Bill Thwaite here.'

Tania smiled at the confident tone in his voice. 'Oh Bill, it's good to hear from you. How's Netta.'

'Grand. They're sending her home. Still icy up with you, I don't doubt. We'll need one of the lads to collect us.'

Her heart fell. She had forgotten that Bill had travelled in the ambulance too and had no transport.

'What's the matter, lass?'

She hated to tell him. 'Andrew's down in the barn. There's been a bit of trouble with the ewes. Neil had a fall and hurt his shoulder. His ankle too.

'He can't put it to the ground. Jake took over from Andrew last night and he's flat out now.'

'Temperature's rising a bit here,' said Bill. 'We'll manage. They'll put on transport, like as not. Or we'll sort something out ourselves. We'll see.'

'I'll go and get Andrew to speak to you, shall I?'

'No need, lass. Keep yourselves warm and fed.'

'Good luck, Bill. I'm so sorry.'

'Not your fault.'

It wasn't her fault, but Tania felt guilty even though they were doing the best they could and Bill understood that. She returned to the kitchen, deep in thought.

She would like to send Gregor down with a message for Andrew, but didn't dare in case the dogs had been let out now.

They finished tidying the kitchen between them. Neil joined them, hobbling his way downstairs and cringing when the corner of the door caught his shoulder.

He was dressed in working jeans and an old sweater as if he planned to be outside with his brother and not in the crowded kitchen deafened by the shrill voices of the girls.

She sent Collette upstairs for the tray and then turned her attention to Neil. His pale face was evidence enough that he was still in pain.

She found some painkillers in her rucksack and made him another hot drink.

★   ★   ★

After the others had gone outside for more sledging Neil allowed her to look at the swelling of his ankle and then apply a cold water compress using a tea towel from the drawer.

'That's fine now,' he said. 'I doubt I've broken it, but we'll see. I'll get it up on a stool in the other room until it eases a bit then I'll be fine.'

She hoped he was right. He looked pleased when she told him that his parents would soon be home when transport could be found, but was doubtful whether it would set out knowing the roads would be difficult up here.

Hope flickered for a moment as she thought of Jake.

'Jake?' she said. 'Could he drive your dad's car?'

Neil shook his head. 'Not insured for anyone else but us.'

She should have thought of that.

'Does Andrew know the position?' Neil said.

She had forgotten Andrew. 'I'll go down and tell him now,' she said.

Hastily she filled a flask with tea and made a couple of cheese sandwiches to take with her.

A Visitor Arrives

When Jake woke a watery sun was breaking through the clouds and illuminating the copper pot on the windowsill with a golden glow.

For a moment he thought a thaw might have set in. But no, he could tell the by the iciness of the room that the temperature outside was still low.

He sprang out of bed, glad that he had left the curtains open when he fell into bed so that he wasn't tempted to doze off again when he should be up and doing things.

He stretched and then looked at his watch. Ten o'clock. He'd slept long enough. Andrew might be in need of more help down there with the ewes and he must check on Tania and the others over at the house and get some food inside him at the same time. With luck Neil might be feeling better after a long rest.

The path to the barn had been treacherous last night, the black ice impossible to see in the dark even in the beam of a torch. He hoped he hadn't sustained any lasting injury.

Downstairs the stove needed attention and he took a moment or two to wonder if anyone had thought the check on the weather forecast.

So far there was no sign of a thaw. Icy patches on the ground outside vied with the mounds of snow shovelled there when the boys were clearing the path.

Outside the air wasn't quite as cold as yesterday, though, and a breeze was stirring the branches of the conifer behind the cottages.

Head down, he moved carefully along the path, wondering at the distant voices, too distant, surely to belong to his charges? Intrigued he crossed to the other side of the yard to look down over the snowy hillside.

Down below, where the road curved to cross the bridge, he could just make out a car at a peculiar angle to the wall, half tipped on one side.

Around it several tiny dark figures were jumping up and down waving their arms about. He couldn't see who they were from this distance, but knew at once that the scene before him was intricately bound up with him and he had to do something about it immediately.

He clambered over the wall and with his long legs made short work of wading down the snowy slope.

For a moment, recognising the car's owner, he was blinded by a red mist that cleared abruptly and left him speechless.

'It's Annie,' Max called out.

He could see that well enough and he was far from pleased to see his cousin standing there at the side of her car looking vulnerable in her black jacket with her glasses half way down her nose.

'Annie, for goodness sake! What do you think you're doing?'

She pushed her glasses back in a familiar gesture. 'I came to see what I could do to help out,' she said defensively.

'And much good that's done in the circumstances,' he snapped. 'Where's Tania? Did she ask you to come?'

'She wasn't there at the farm. This lot were and they came to help me out. I had to leave the car and walk.'

'So where is she?'

Annie shrugged. 'Don't ask me. Gone with Ivan I shouldn't wonder, sick to death of your bad temper.'

He took a deep breath, conscious of Max's pale anxious face and Becky's trembling lips. 'Get off back up there, all of you and look sharp about it,' he ordered. 'Gregor, stay here. I'll need your help.'

The boy looked as if he would like to escape too.

'Have you got sacking in the boot or anything else for the wheels to get a grip?'

Annie shook her head. 'I didn't know

it would be like this.'

'Obviously not.' He looked round and saw nothing of any use. 'We'll have to leave the car here if we can get it upright and out of the middle of the road.'

'I know,' said Annie in a subdued tone. She shivered. 'I only wanted to help.'

Ignoring her, Jake indicated with a nod of his head that Gregor should join him in heaving the car into a better position. With the brake off the three of them pushed it to a suitable place and then Jake leaned in and applied the handbrake.

'Safe enough there for the moment,' he said. 'Go off and join the others now, Gregor, and make sure you all stick around the farmyard.'

He watched them all trudge back up the hill.

Annie at his side said nothing and for a fraction of a second he felt a glimmer of sympathy for her but then reality set in. 'You'd no business roping them in to

209

help,' he said. 'Tania should have had more sense than to let you.'

'I told you she wasn't there,' said Annie with spirit. 'And she doesn't know I've come either. The car was in the way of anything that wanted to get past and I couldn't move it on my own. Have some sense, Jake.'

She reached into the boot for her holdall and then shut the lid with a decisive bang and locked the car. 'You might at least look pleased to see me.'

'Pleased?' Jake said in astonishment. 'Haven't I enough problems without you turning up getting in the way?'

Annie heaved up her bag and glared at him. 'Tania said there were problems so I came prepared with all the medical stuff I could lay my hands on.

'Don't tell me there's nobody in need of a nurse's attention. If not I'll be sorely tempted to do something drastic to change that immediately.'

'You always were a firebrand, Annie.'

'And I've not changed now.'

His lips twitched. What was done was

done. 'You'd better come up to the house,' he said.

On the way up the snowy field he filled her in on the details of what was turning out to be a fiasco of a challenge.

'And you can't cope with failure, can you Jake?' she said.

He stopped walking and swung round to face her. 'What do you mean?'

'Jake the Achiever,' she said. 'Good at everything you take on. You can't bear the thought that you could ever be mistaken.'

'That's not true.'

'No?' She looked at him over the top of her glasses and smiled so kindly that he bit back the retort that had sprung to his lips.

They set off again, trudging up through snow that was crisp underfoot and gave few signs of thawing.

'Tell me, Annie,' he said slowly. 'I know that Tania and Max's mother died some months ago. Do you mind telling me how it came about?'

211

'I don't know why I should tell you. Why do you want to know anyway?'

'Annie . . . please?'

She looked at him sternly. 'Idle curiosity?'

'No, no. Of course not. It really matters that I should know this.'

She hesitated and then made up her mind suddenly. 'If you promise not to snap at me in your unpleasant way I'll tell you since you look so downcast. It was a terrible time for them all. She was expecting a baby and something went tragically wrong. That's all. She died and so did the unborn baby.'

'I see.'

They walked in silence for a few moments, Jake deep in thought.

'And I didn't mean it about Tania going off with Ivan,' Annie said at last, puffing a little.

'Ivan?'

'I knew she'd have more sense once she'd finished with him. I'm sure about that. Once you've made up your mind about someone, that's it in my book.'

Jake frowned, but said nothing.

They had reached the top of the field now and were about to clamber over the wall into the yard. He got over first and took her bag from her. With her short legs she needed help, but at last she was over, breathing fast with the exertion.

'I'm glad it's not me on this walk of yours,' she said. 'Me too,' he said.

★ ★ ★

Tania, on her way back to the house from the barn, caught sight of Jake talking to someone on the other side of the yard and stopped in surprise. Annie . . . surely not?

'Tania!' Annie cried and then came rushing towards her, arms out-stretched and caught hold of her in a tight hug. 'Where were you when I needed you?'

'Oh Annie, it's so good to see you.'

Annie's glasses had slipped down her

213

nose again and she pushed them back, laughing.

Jake stood a little apart, regarding them both.

Suddenly Tania realised that he knew nothing of Bill's phone call or that Neil's ankle was causing trouble. She had left Andrew sorting things out down below, pleased that for the moment the worry over the ewes was over.

There were, of course, plenty of other things needing his attention, but now that Jake had surfaced Andrew might well be free to do as his father had requested and collect his parents from hospital.

Before she could say anything Jake handed Annie her bag. 'Enough of this,' he said. 'You'd better make yourself useful, Annie.'

He turned and made for the barn.

'He's got no finer feelings, my crabby cousin,' said Annie as she watched him go. 'I don't know how you put up with him. I bet he's harrying the lot of you all the time.'

At that moment sounds of loud cheering and shrieks of laughter filled the air.

'They've made a sledging course over there,' Tania said.

'I must say they sound pretty happy,' said Annie.

Tania smiled. 'They've been great.'

'But Jake's still got a long face on him, wanting his own way no doubt.'

'It's not like that, said Tania in quick defence. 'He's got the interests of the boys and girls at heart. It means a lot to them, completing the challenge he set them.'

'Says who?'

'It's good for their sense of worth, you see.'

Annie gave a scornful laugh. 'You can't fool me, my friend. It's as plain as anything you've fallen for that cantankerous man and won't hear the slightest thing against him.'

Tania felt herself flush. 'It's not like that. I'm being fair, that's all.'

215

'Oh yeah?'

'Jake's right. There are things to do,' said Tania with a firmness she didn't feel. 'Are you coming in the house or not?'

'You've Got Jake'

'By, it's hot in here.' Annie threw off her jacket, removed her steamed-up glasses and wiped them on the welt of her jersey.

'That can't do them much good. Here, use this.'

Tania tore off a paper towel from the roll by the sink and handed it to her. Then she took her winter outer garments off and pushed the kettle onto the hot plate.

Annie was looking round the comfortable room with interest. 'You seem to have made yourself at home here, my friend. What's the elder son like?'

'Neil?' Tania laughed. 'A big farmer who's gentle with animals.'

'Aww. He sounds lovely.'

'For you or for me?'

'For me, of course. You've got Jake.'

Tania turned quickly away and busied herself putting tea bags into the pot. She didn't want any arguments about that at the moment. 'You can check Neil out for yourself if you want,' she said. 'He's in the sitting room with his swollen ankle up on a footstool. He had a fall on the ice last night. He hurt his shoulder too.'

Annie's eyes glittered. 'I'll just check,' she said.

Neil put down the magazine he was reading and tried to struggle up.

'Stay where you are,' Annie said at her most autocratic. 'Tania tells me you've injured yourself.'

A flush spread across his strong features. 'Nothing that can't be put right with a bit of rest.'

'Annie's a nurse,' Tania said, feeling sorry for him.

'A friend of yours?'

She nodded. 'She's quite safe even if she doesn't look it.'

Annie pursed her lips as she eyed the

rather clumsy tea towel compress on his ankle.

'I did my best,' said Tania. 'Not good enough?'

'Like me to take a look, Neil?' Annie said. 'I've brought my bag.'

Neil, looking hunted, nodded.

Tania rushed to fetch the black holdall that Annie had brought with her. By the time she got back Annie had the makeshift bandage off and was kneeling on the hearthrug and examining Neil's ankle with a professional eye.

'Hopefully it looks worse than it is,' she said. She ran her fingers over the injured ankle, making Neil wince. 'Could you get a bowl of cold water, Tania? You did a good job, but it needs renewing.'

By the time Tania was back for the second time Annie had unpacked a crêpe bandage from her bag and was deep in conversation with Neil about losing control of her car up by the bridge and it almost turning right over.

She made it sound so amusing that

Neil was smiling now, leaning forward in his chair and telling her what she should have done to avoid getting stuck on that blind bend.

'I'll make some tea,' said Tania and escaped to the kitchen.

She sank down at the table, glad of a few moments to herself. Annie's arrival was definitely a blessing.

She had cheered Neil up already. Even her cousin, Jake, might relax a little and stop acting like a coiled spring. But she didn't know how Annie would fit in here and what Bill's reaction would be at someone else getting in on the act.

A vision shot into her mind of Jake's hurt expression when she refused to go on from Slough Fell and then of his anger at having to admit defeat because he needed her with them for the sake of the girls in the party.

She could hardly believe, now, that she had done this when she knew how much it would hurt him.

The lid of the kettle began to rattle

and she stared at it as if she had never seen it before. What her friend had hinted about her feelings for Jake was disturbing.

She was being loyal to him that was all, sorry for his deep disappointment that his plans weren't turning out as he had expected. How could Annie have picked up anything different from the short time she had seen them together?

The scraping of boots outside the door made her jump to her feet, awkward at the thought of Jake's presence at this moment. Confused, she saw Andrew come in.

He grinned at her. 'All well up here too?'

She nodded and went to the stove to push the clattering kettle off the heat. 'My friend's here. She's looking at Neil's ankle.'

'Oh aye? That's grand then. I'll take a shower now and then get off to collect the parents. Jake's doing a bit of tidying up down there. He'll be up soon when he's shut Stinker and Bob in their quarters. I'll phone Dad and put him in the picture.'

His cheerfulness was catching. She smiled as she made the tea. In the sitting room Neil's ankle was up on the footstool and Annie was sitting on the hearthrug as close to the crackling fire as she could. The two of them looked so companionable that Tania poured a cup of tea for herself and left them to it.

A Bitter Exchange

The knock on the back door made Tania jump. For a confused moment she didn't move. Then the knock came again. She opened the door.

'Ivan?' She should have known. He had spent last night down in Gillerthwaite promising to return for her today when she had come to her senses.

He came in looking quietly confident. 'My car's outside ready and waiting, Tania,' he said. 'Now you've had time to consider you'll know it makes sense to come back with me.'

Senses again. She felt a smile on her lips and quickly banished it. She had come to her senses about Ivan before she had even left home.

'So I take it you're packed and ready?'

Stunned at his self-assurance, she shook her head. 'No Ivan, I told you

223

yesterday. I'm needed here.' Even as she said it she realised that this wasn't entirely true now, but he wasn't to know that the capable Annie had turned up raring to go. It was fortunate that she had abandoned her car down by the bridge.

'What can I do to convince you, Ivan?' she said.

She backed towards the Aga as he stepped towards her. At the same time she heard the rattle of the latch and saw Jake in the doorway.

'Jake?' Confused, she felt sudden warmth flood her face.

He looked grim as he came in and slammed the door behind him. 'And who's this?'

Ivan swung round and moved away a little.

'An old friend,' Tania said, feeling at fault in being caught in a situation not of her own making. 'Ivan. He was worried about me.'

'Worried? In what way?'

'That's obvious, surely?' Ivan said

with a smile. 'The conditions up here in the Dales have been horrific these last few days. Hardly suitable for tramping through with a bunch of children.'

Jake glowered. 'And exactly what business is it of yours?'

'I care, that's all, as anyone would who has Tania's interest at heart.'

Tania took a deep breath, alarmed at the way things were going. 'Ivan, it's all right. I told you. We're staying here at the farm for another couple of days.'

'You're not serious?'

She felt Jake's eyes on her, but dare not look at him. 'Quite serious. I'll be all right, Ivan, I promise.'

He looked unconvinced. 'But you know I've come all this way to take you home, Tania. Your brother, too, of course, and anyone else who wants to come.'

'We're as right as rain here, Ivan. You can see that. There's nothing for you to worry about.'

'I'm not so sure about that.'

'Didn't you hear what the girl said?'

Jake's voice was deadly quiet.

'Only too well, but I'll not believe it. She's just feeling responsible for everyone, that's all.'

'You think so?' Jake's voice was icy.

Ivan smiled. 'Don't deny it, Tania. I can see the way things are going.'

Speechless at his assumption, she gazed at him. She wanted to convince him once and for all how wrong he was, but the words wouldn't come.

Jake moved towards an empty log basket placed ready for him to fill and take back to the cottage. He picked it up, looking as if he could easily find another use for it if provoked further.

'We need to talk, Tania,' he said. 'Our plans have to be finalised if that is your wish.' Only the tightness of his lips betrayed his effort to control his temper.

She nodded. 'I understand.' But did she? This was all getting a bit much for her. She wanted Ivan away from here but felt too weak to make it happen.

'I hope so.' The faint gleam in Jake's

eyes instead of the coldness she feared sent a shimmer of surprise through her. 'I won't allow anyone to be taken off by someone I don't know. Get rid of him, Tania, or I will.'

'I'm astonished you let him speak of you like that,' said Ivan. 'I thought better of you, Tania. Where's your spirit?'

She threw back her head. 'Deep inside where it always is.'

'Out!' Jake ordered.

Such was the hostility in his voice that Ivan took a step back. 'I don't believe you want this, Tania. You have only to say the word. You have my mobile number.'

Jake shot her an enigmatic look as he moved to the door. 'I'll leave you to make your decision, Tania. A lot depends on it. I'll not be far away.'

She stared at the closed door with a feeling of wonder and for a magical second allowed herself to hope Jake's expression meant more than his words indicated.

'That's that then,' Ivan said with satisfaction.

His triumph roused something in her that immediately strengthened her. 'I'm not coming home with you, Ivan,' she said. 'I've made my mind up and am going to stick to it.'

'But why not?' He looked so intense she was startled. 'That obnoxious chap has really got to you, hasn't he?'

She held herself in with difficulty, struggling to stay calmly determined. 'I'm truly sorry, Ivan. I don't want to come with you, now or ever. I wish I knew what to say that doesn't sound cruel but I really mean it.'

There was silence.

She stood with her back to the draining board, feeling the unit pressing against her body. Ivan had shown concern for her safety. He was a kind man, but understandably bitter at her reaction and her heart felt full at his obvious hurt. 'I'm sorry,' she said again, less brusquely this time.

'You're sorry?'

She knew that she could never make Ivan understand the loyalty she now felt towards Jake's project and all the youngsters out there in the snow. Not in a million years.

She was shaken by the knowledge that she would give Jake her support, not by running away, but by remaining here on his behalf until they were no longer needed. They would make their own way home by whatever route he chose. Then what ever happened after that she would be able go on with her life a better person because of it.

'You should be on your way now, Ivan,' she said. 'Thank you for coming. I'll never forget your kindness.'

It had taken Ivan's unexpected presence here at Slough Fell to confirm for her that Jake's dreams were her dreams too. Her gratitude to Ivan for her profound certainty was deep.

'And that's all you've got to say?'

Without a word he grabbed his jacket and strode to the door without looking at her again.

She closed it behind him and stood leaning on it, tense with exhaustion, until she heard his car engine start up.

He was gone and the relief was stupefying. But dare she believe he had gone out of her life for good and wasn't merely waiting at Miss Crabbe's place to take his chance again another time?

Here in the farm kitchen the silence was shattering. She closed her eyes and rested her head in her hands. This was an important moment in her life. She had a made a decision and would stick with it. It was the right thing to do.

A Choice is Made

For a short time Jake stood in the yard until the sight of the parked car that could be the means of taking Tania out of his life was more than he could bear.

Then he walked a short way along to the path to the cottage and paused in the shelter of a wall, too weak suddenly to go move on until he felt calmer.

He heard the door of the house open and close and the vehicle drive off. Returning to the kitchen had to be done and the sooner the better. He didn't move.

The accustomed chilliness of the air on his face was lessening a little now and in the lifting of the intense cold tiny drops of melting ice began to trickle from the wall onto the path beneath. A thaw at last, but it had come too late to continue the walk over the top to the next dale because he had to be back at his desk the day after tomorrow. It couldn't be done.

He heard the sound of another vehicle. Andrew leaving for the hospital . . .

He became aware that he hadn't seen the boys and girls yet this morning and there was no sound of voices now. Then he caught sight of Gregor making for the cottage and called out to him. When there was no response he wondered if in his present dreamlike state he was invisible. Somehow it ceased to matter.

* * *

Sounds of excitement outside had Tania leaping up and rushing for the door, her tiredness forgotten. Collete and Wayne almost fell inside followed by a scared-looking Becky.

'Who was that man who was here?' Collete demanded, her cheeks rosy and her eyes glowing.

'We thought he was going to take Aussie away,' said Wayne.

'It's all right. He's gone now. He's not taken Aussie with him. Why should he?' said Tania. 'But where's Gregor? And Max? He hasn't gone down to the barn?'

'Gregor went off to find Jake,' said Collette. She pulled off her woolly hat and her abundant hair cascaded down her back.

'Max has taken Aussie somewhere to keep him safe,' said Wayne.

'But that's silly,' said Tania. 'You'd better go and get him back.'

'We can't,' said Becky. 'We don't know where he went.'

'How long ago was this?'

They looked at each other and Collette shrugged. 'Max and Aussie went off as soon as that man came.'

Heart churning, Tania considered. How long ago was that? Half an hour? No need to panic. She glanced at her watch. She stared helplessly at Wayne and the girls. 'Why didn't you tell me before?'

'The man might have taken Aussie,' said Wayne.

'I told you, Ivan didn't come for the dog,' she said sharply.

'We didn't know that,' said Becky.

Tania took a painful breath. Calm down, she told herself. Max was hiding somewhere to keep Aussie safe. That was all. He would be back soon.

They all jumped as the phone rang in the hall.

Bill Thwaite's deep Yorkshire boomed down the line as Tania picked up the receiver. 'Andrew phoned to say he's on his way, lass,' he said. 'All grand in the barn. Mothers and twins doing well and the others in fine fettle. We'll not be long.'

She bit back the temptation to spill out her worries about her brother. It wouldn't help matters and Max might even be on his way back by now.

'That's good, Bill.'

'The road's passable. We'll be with you in under an hour.'

'Who was that?' asked Becky, round-eyed, when Tania returned to the kitchen.

'Bill. They'll be back soon,' she said. 'You lot stay here. I'll go down to the barn and see if Max is down that way.'

She sloshed across the yard, praying she would find him there. Although the yard was clear of snow the surrounding fields and hills shone white in the lowering sky.

She shivered, feeling a slight drizzle in the air. She heard slow movements from inside the barn as she opened the door enough to check if Max was there.

There was a shout from the open door of the house and Tania's heart quickened in hope as Wayne came bounding out to greet her.

'Is Max back?' she called.

'Jake's here,' he said, breathlessly. 'He's looks mad.'

Tania hastened forward, stumbling on the wet cobbles, close to tears at seeing Jake standing there.

He stared at her in such a piercing

way she felt alarmed. Surely he didn't think she would go with Ivan? But she couldn't cope with that now. 'Max has gone missing,' she blurted out.

'So how did that come about?'

She shivered with guilt for not taking more care of her brother. Then she raised her head, struggling to sound positive as she told him what had happened. Gregor was the problem boy, not Max.

His eyes moved thoughtfully over her face. She hoped he would think it was the wind making her eyes water.

'So our first job is to find your brother,' he said. 'Where is everybody?'

A new kind of unease swept over Tania. They were safe in the kitchen, or so she thought. That's where she had told them to stay when she went off to the barn, but she wasn't sure of anything anymore.

She followed him inside where the girls and Wayne were huddled by the Aga in their outdoor clothes. All three looked anxious.

'Gregor didn't come in here with us,' said Becky, cringing back as if he would hit her. 'We don't know where he went. And Max is lost . . . ' She broke off, rubbing her gloved hands across her tearful face.

'Come on, the lot of you, outside,' he ordered.

Collette rammed her hat back as they rushed to obey.

Jake banged shut the door behind himself and Tania and stared up the track to the road, his eyes narrowed.

'Gregor must have decided to go on by himself,' he said. 'What's wrong with the boy? We both knew there were likely to be snow drifts further up.'

'Shall we go and get him back?' asked Collette eagerly.

'Go up to the first bend and check if you can see him' said Jake. He can't have gone far.'

Tania found she was trembling and struggled hard to control it. 'And Max?' she whispered.

'We'll find him,' Jake said and the

kind note in his voice was almost her undoing. 'We'll start searching down the slope over the wall. I'd go that way if I wanted to hide a dog for a while. How about you?'

She gulped and tried to smile, appreciating his attempts to lighten the situation. 'If you say so.'

'Good girl.'

He made it seem simple, but she couldn't believe that finding Max would be that easy in the bleak wastes that stretched downhill as far as she could see. The many snowy dips and hollows could hide anyone for hours especially if they had fallen and hurt themselves. 'Oh Max,' she whispered.

'Max!' Jake shouted so suddenly she jumped.

The sound of his voice faded and there was no reply. He called again and then climbed on top of the wall to peer into the distance.

An Understanding

The yells and cat calls from the others became louder as they came streaming down the track to join them.

'A car's coming!' Collette yelled. 'And we couldn't see Gregor.'

Bill's huge Land Rover came slowly towards them. It pulled up by the door and Andrew leapt out of the driving seat.

Without a flicker of surprise he looked across at Jake poised on the wall with his body outlined against the bleak sky. 'There you are,' he said as if he had expected to see him there 'All well here?'

Jake jumped down from the wall. 'Tania's young brother's taken your dog, Aussie, off to hide him. He was afraid that someone had come to take him away.'

'Nothing but a nuisance that dog,'

said Andrew laconically.

'Max loves Aussie,' said Tania in a broken voice. 'And now they've both gone off and we don't know where they are.'

'They'll be fine, never fear,' said Andrew with confidence. 'This'll bring the dog and the little lad back, I shouldn't wonder.' He put two fingers in his mouth and let forth such a piercing whistle that the hills rang with it.

Jake shot Tania a glance filled with reassurance. 'If Max is the boy I think he is he'll be back before we know it.'

Andrew blew another high-pitched whistle into the still air, let the sound sink into the silence before whistling again. Far away they heard a dog bark.

'Aussie?' said Tania with hope in her voice. She clutched Jake's arm, hardly knowing what she was doing.

'That's Aussie,' said Andrew in satisfaction.

He turned to help his mother out of the back of the car. Then Bill was out too, waving at everyone and giving the thumbs up sign.

'I'll need to get back down about the place,' said Andrew, sternness in his voice now that didn't fool Tania in the least.

Like his father and his brother his emotions ran deep but weren't to be shared with the rest of the world.

Tania waved to Netta as she went into the house and then moved forward to climb over the wall, but Jake held her back.

'You'll do no good over there,' he said. 'Max'll come in his own good time.'

She felt her blood tingle as they waited.

They heard distant voices now, shouting for the dog to slow down. Could it really be?' She lifted a radiant face to Jake. 'I can hear two of them. Max and *Gregor*?'

'We'll soon see,' Jake said his voice tense.

At last they saw them, Max holding

Aussie tightly by his collar and Gregor alongside, stumbling up the hill towards them with their heads down.

'Oh Max!' Tania cried.

'I found him,' Gregor said, scrambling over the wall.

Aussie leapt over into the yard too, shaking snow from his black and white body, wagging his tail hard and looking decidedly pleased with himself.

Tania rushed to Max longing to hug him, but knowing he wouldn't want it, managed to stop herself just in time. 'Oh Max!' she said, her voice so weak he hardly heard her.

'That man, has he gone?' Max said.

'I promise you he's gone and he won't come back,' Tania said fervently.

'You gave me your solemn promise not to go missing again, Gregor,' Jake said sharply. 'So what went wrong?'

Gregor's eyes widened for an instant, then his shoulders shot up and he held his chin high. 'Max was miles away, down in the hollow by the river,' he said gruffly. 'He didn't know how to get back.'

'You went to look for Max knowing he had the dog with him?' said Tania, full of wonder at his bravery.

'It's bad being lost.'

'But why *you*, Gregor?' said Jake.

For a second Gregor looked deflated, then he braced himself. His eyes flashed from Tania to the tall man gazing at him so speculatively. 'Someone had to do it,' he said. 'I managed all right, didn't I?'

'I'm proud of you, lad,' said Jake quietly.

Gregor seemed to grow a couple of inches and to tower above the rest of the group gathering round Max and Aussie.

The dog was loving it, jumping up and licking as many faces as he could reach.

In the excitement Jake stood a little apart with one hand on Gregor's shoulder as if he couldn't quite believe the way events were unfolding.

Tania, too, felt bemused. 'You're brave, Gregor,' she said. 'I'm so thankful you knew what to do and did it.'

'It was great seeing you, Gregor,' said Max. 'But I'm fine, Tania, really I am and so is Aussie.'

'We can see you are, lad,' Jake said heartily.

'You won't let Aussie be taken away will you?' said Max, gazing up at him.

'No way, lad,' said Jake. 'You can let Aussie go now.'

As Max let go of the collar Gregor moved swiftly to stand behind Jake. Tania, knowing that Gregor's fear of dogs would never completely go away and understanding why, went to stand beside him for support.

'Let's get inside,' said Jake. 'We need to thaw out, especially you boys.'

Tania's heart felt so full she could hardly look at Jake. She marvelled that he was here, that Max was back and that it was Gregor who had played a big part in that.

'Gregor's a good lad,' she said huskily

as they all crowded into the kitchen ahead of them.

'He's had a tough time throughout his short life,' said Jake. 'I forced him to come on this challenge because I thought that was what he needed and he would gain something from it. I admit I had doubts when his behaviour seemed to prove I was wrong.'

'You were right, Jake,' she said.

'I've felt my responsibilities towards him lying rather too heavily at times.'

'But not now. Not anymore. This will have been the making of him.'

'I hope so.'

She wanted to say that anyone's life would be enhanced by Jake's presence in it because that was how she felt. But it wouldn't do. She looked up at him and saw a brightness in his eyes that sent a thrill through her.

He smiled briefly. 'But now there are things to be done,' he said. 'We'll need to get them all round the table and put them in the picture about Netta and our position here.'

Tania's eyes watered in the sudden warmth of the crowded kitchen as they joined the others. The table lamp on the dresser shone out in welcome even though it was only mid morning. Suddenly she remembered that Jake hadn't eaten today.

There was a sound in the doorway from the hall and Annie came in.

'Annie?' said Tania in surprise. 'I'd forgotten you were here.'

Annie's eyes moved from Jake to Tania. 'I can see why,' she said.

Tania felt herself flush and turned quickly to pick up one of the discarded jackets that had slithered off its hook.

Annie flopped down at the table and sat with her elbows on it and her chin resting in her hands. 'I never did get that tea,' she said.

Wayne sprang up. 'I'll make it.'

There was a scurry of activity from Wayne and Becky. Cereal was produced for Jake and biscuits for the rest of them.

Andrew returned with another basket filled with logs to carry into the sitting room. 'Mum'll do right well in there,' he said.

Bill came into the kitchen then, smiling broadly at them all. 'She'll want to see you when she's properly settled.'

Tania smiled. 'I'll get some tea made for her, shall I?'

'You do that, lass.'

Tania poured boiling water into the small tea pot and placed it on the tray. 'Take this in to her,' she said.

'I will that.'

He nodded at Max, shivering by the Aga. 'Plenty of hot water for showers for those that need it. The young lad looks fair starved.'

★ ★ ★

Later, when they all crowded into the sitting room to greet Netta she looked across at Gregor, a serious expression on her face. 'I've been hearing about your bravery, lad. If you don't mind, when the baby comes we'd like to call him Gregor.'

Gregor's face was expressionless and for an incredulous moment Tania thought he would burst into tears. Then he swallowed and stood up straight looking quickly at Jake and then away again.

'What if he's a girl?' he said, his voice gruff.

Netta smiled. 'Then we'll have to think about that.'

With that the tension broke and everyone laughed.

'Gregorina?' suggested Collette, giggling. 'Gregette?'

'Gregora?' Annie said.

'We'd better take good care to have a lad then,' said Bill, a twinkle in his eye.

Tania smiled at the happy scene. 'Time's getting on,' she said. 'I'll get something out for lunch, Shall I?'

'Thanks, lass.' Bill got to his feet. 'You've enough young helpers. If Annie here will stay with Netta and Neil, I'll be right glad. I'll take Jake off for a while. We'll have a walk round outside and see what's what, lad. We've some talking to do.'

Without anything being said everyone seemed to accept that they would be on the way home next day. After lunch had been eaten and cleared away Wayne and Becky peeled potatoes and carrots for the evening meal and then settled themselves at the kitchen table happily sorting through a box of indoor games watched over by Gregor.

Collette, anxious to be outside making the most of what snow was left, persuaded Max to come out with her.

'Can I, Tania?' he said as she returned from the freezer in the barn with four packs of sausages. 'Aussie's out there and I want to check he's safe.'

She looked at her brother's eager face and smiled. 'Of course, Max.'

Biting her tongue to prevent herself uttering words of caution she watched him go. Fussing over him was the last thing Max wanted and something she must learn not to do from now on in spite of her recent fright.

Since Annie was in her nursing element in the sitting room and there was nothing else needing her attention for the moment she was free to go out too.

They had arrived at Slough Fell Farm by a different route over the top of the fell and she wanted to see how far she could get by heading up the road in the other direction and seeing what lay ahead.

The ground underfoot had been cleared of snow but the banks on either side of the track were still white like the fields. She set off briskly, glad to be in the open air. The sense of freedom was exhilarating.

Where the track met the road she paused to look back at the farm buildings. This would make a good photo and a reminder of their time here.

She pulled her camera out of her pocket and raised it to her eyes, surprised to notice a movement down below.

She knew at once it was Jake because of his swift stride as he came to join her. Her heart quickened to see him.

He smiled as he reached her. 'Shall we walk on a bit?' he said.

'I was going further up the road and see what it's like up there.'

'An excellent idea.'

In companionable silence they walked up the road. She was reminded of when they had started to clear a path from the bunkhouse to the farm and she had felt an extraordinary sense of nearness to him.

'This snow will have gone in a few days,' he said.

She nodded. Mourning its passing was odd when it had caused so many problems. But although the snow had prevented their completing what they had set out to do it had given them so much more.

The road topped the hill and they paused to survey the snowy wilderness that stretched before them. Here and there a boundary wall showed stark

251

against the white and in the distance she saw a group of conifers that probably sheltered more farm buildings. She pulled her camera out again and focussed.

Jake took a deep appreciative breath. 'Great, isn't it?' he said. 'There's the feeling that nature is surging beneath all this just biding its time to burst forth. There's rightness about it, a sense of fulfilment.'

Thoughtfully she replaced her camera. His words had an added truth for her because it was Jake who voiced them.

'I can see why you love it and want to give others the same feeling of connection with the landscape that you have,' she said.

'It's important that we never lose that.' He spoke quietly and she knew that this was the true essence of the man.

She had learnt so much about him these last few days. She felt humbled that he was talking to her like this as if he wanted to be certain of her understanding of his deepest feelings.

She smiled, aware that he understood that now.

There was a pool of melted snow near the side of the road. Jake picked up a pebble and dropped it. The stone fell with a splash, disturbing the surface of the tawny water in a satisfying way.

'Bill and I had a long talk,' he said. 'We see eye to eye on a lot of things and he has a few ideas he wants to run past me.'

'Architectural ones?'

He glanced at her, smiling. 'Could be.'

'That's good, isn't it?'

'Very good.'

'Does it mean that he'd like you to help him with plans for expanding the buildings?'

Jake looked thoughtfully down at the trickle of melted snow dripping into the pool of water. Then he nodded but didn't enlarge on how exactly this could be done.

'It's the possibility of having a dream

come true that makes a life interesting. Don't you think, Tania?' he said. 'I dream of helping these youngsters come to terms with their lives. The sense of achievement and self-worth of all of them, especially of Gregor, has increased amazingly these last few days and that's largely down to you.'

'Me?' she said in surprise.

He smiled as they turned to retrace their steps. 'I should have listened to you when you pointed out that the sense of achievement I wanted for them was right here at Slough Fell. Apart from the bad weather conditions we were needed here. I see that now. My personal challenge was to accept that.'

'Mine too when I hated hurting you,' she said quietly.

He looked at her closely. 'Are you all right, Tania? You look pale. I know you've had a hard time lately, but it seems that Netta is going to be all right.'

She felt drowned in his penetrating

gaze and for a moment couldn't speak. A hard time? What had Annie been saying?

'Not to mention the shock of Max going missing.'

She took a deep breath. 'I'm fine,' she said at last. 'And Max is too.'

'He's a good lad.'

'He loves it here as much as I do. There's something about this place that seems to sing out to me.'

'Bill has a good head on his shoulders,' he said. 'You don't have to be back at work till next week, I believe? He's planning to ask you if you and Max would stay on for a few days when the rest of us leave tomorrow. How would you feel about that?'

She was taken aback. How did she feel? He sounded as if he thought this an excellent plan now that they were about to be on their way at last, all of them except herself and Max.

He didn't mind about leaving her behind. She felt abandoned and aware of a profound sense of loss. But how could she let him see this? She threw her shoulders back and gazed ahead, unwilling to meet his gaze.

She forced her mind on Max, the young brother who needed her care and who loved it here. He would jump at the chance of staying.

'And Annie?' she managed to get out.

Jake smiled. 'Ah yes, Annie. They'll get her car out of trouble and up to the farm later on. No problem there. She's free this week, too, and if she stays as well she can drive you home at the weekend.'

It was a sensible arrangement. But she didn't want to be sensible when she was weeping inside because Jake's calm acceptance of this practical scheme had wounded her.

She nodded and walked at his side back the farm where she knew they were doing a good job because the Thwaite family needed them.

She had no real idea of how they got there.

Grand Plans

With the boys back in the cottage for the night and her original room vacant again there was no problem with Annie's accommodation.

'I didn't think to bring a sleeping bag,' Annie said, her voice mournful, as she helped Tania raid the linen cupboard on the landing and make up the spare bed.

'I was born to be silly. What did I think I was doing setting out into the wilds without adequate provision? Jake'll be mad at me.'

'Not to worry,' said Tania as she tucked in the blankets. 'He's got other things to think about. And Netta's so pleased to have you here she's only too glad to provide bedding. We can see to the laundry before we leave on Saturday.'

Jake wouldn't be mad, she thought.

Annie was useful taxi driver-material so that she and Max could remain behind at Slough Fell. Because of it, he and the others could leave tomorrow with a clear conscience.

Annie cheered up at once and after the meal of sausages and mash with ten of them squashed round the kitchen table she was her usual optimistic self.

She and Neil between them organised some guessing games in the sitting room after Netta had retired early to bed while Bill and Andrew had a last look around outside. Then Jake joined Bill and his son in the farm office for some business talk. Her heart aching, Tania imagined them enjoying themselves discussing plans.

She leaned back in her chair, her face glowing in the warmth of the logs crackling in the sitting room grate, feeling only part of the scene in front of her. It had been a hectic day, emotionally draining, and her eyelids began to droop. For while she tried to fight it, but it was no use.

She woke with a start to discover that the fire had died down to embers glowing faintly in the hearth. The boys were no longer there and Annie and the girls were playing a card game at the table, their heads bent over their hands and concentrating hard. Tania stretched and sat up, the creak of her chair alerting Annie.

She pushed her glasses further up her nose and looked round. 'You seemed so comfortable in that chair Jake said not to wake you,' she said. 'We won't be long. We're just finishing this game.'

It was soon over and when Collette and Becky had gone off to bed Annie came and plonked herself down on the hearthrug and sat with her hands round her knees. 'Jake says he plans an early start tomorrow,' she said. 'Are you OK, Tania?'

Tania nodded, feeling far from sure. This was their last evening and she should have been making the most of the company not sleeping soundly by the fire. She was hurt too, that Jake hadn't wanted to wish her goodnight.

Even when she was in bed and listening to Annie's even breathing Tania couldn't forget it. Even if that moment of standing with him earlier looking into the distance across miles of snowy wilderness meant nothing to him, the memory of it would stay with forever.

She sighed, turned over and pulled her sleeping bag up round her neck. Slough Fell Farm that had given them generous and welcoming refuge when they needed it and would seem bereft when Jake and his charges were no longer in it.

Sleep was a long time in coming and when it did was full of fractured dreams of dogs and barren hillsides over-run by vehicles that churned the snow beneath their wheels to ugly slush.

★ ★ ★

Tania looked out on a grey world when she pulled the bedroom curtains aside

260

next morning. The thaw was well under way now and melting snow dripped from the roof and ran in wavy rivulets down the windowpane.

Annie's bed was empty and there were sounds of movement from the girls' room.

Neil hobbled down to join them at breakfast, looking pleased with himself. Bill and Andrew came in from outside, shrugging off their heavy outdoor gear and moving to the Aga for warmth.

Annie slid past them to take a plate of toast and marmalade up to Netta and then came down again saying she was enjoying her rest, but was planning to be up by the time Bill left with Jake and his charges to transport them to the place where Jake's Land Rover would be waiting for them.

'But that's miles away,' said Max, wide-eyed. 'It'll take *hours*.'

Bill smiled his slow smile. 'Nay, lad, Not in Slough Fell's magic vehicle.'

Max stared at him with his cereal spoon halfway to his lips.

'The road goes straight there, keeping to the lower ground,' Tania explained. 'We came a longer more circular route over the fells.'

'But why?' said Max.

'You may well ask,' said Annie, reaching for the marmalade.

Gregor scowled at her. 'Don't you know why?' he said.

'It seems you do,' said Jake pleasantly.

Annie looked at Gregor over the top of her glasses. 'Tell me then, Gregor.'

'We needed something hard to do to prove we're not softies,' he said proudly. 'We can cope with anything.' He took a bite out of his toast as if he had said enough to convince her.

And he probably had, Tania thought. More than anyone, Gregor had gained tremendously from the last few days.

She smiled at him as he sat there, head down, making the most of his last meal at the farm.

Then she looked away and caught Jake's eyes on her. 'We'll soon need to make a move,' he said.

She shivered, hoping no-one had noticed. She would be glad now when he had gone and the parting was over.

After that there was a rush of activity as the last of the packing was done and rucksacks assembled outside the door. Ten o'clock was striking on the kitchen clock before they were ready to set off.

Collette gave Tania such a tremendous hug that she was nearly lifted off her feet. Becky looked sad as she stood there in her navy jacket zipped to the neck and her fair hair scraped back from her face with a black headband.

'Goodbye, Becky and you, too, Wayne,' Tania said, a lump in her throat. 'It's been great knowing you all.'

Wayne, looking suddenly wan too, stood a little to one side. Gregor was already in Bill's vehicle glaring out at Aussie standing quietly with Max's hand on his collar.

Then Jake was at her side. He looked at her in silence for a long moment and then smiled briefly. 'Goodbye, Tania.

Look after yourself and the others too. Until Saturday.'

Her breath caught in her throat. Saturday, she thought. Not today with the rest of them and Jake. As if she needed reminding.

'Goodbye, Jake,' she said. 'And thank you.' Now why had she added something so meaningless?

The answering gleam in his eyes startled her, but there was no time to wonder about it now.

They stood in the yard watching as Bill's vehicle filled to overflowing with his cargo of five bodies and their luggage.

Then it drove slowly up the track to the road and they could see it no more.

There was a moment of desolation. Then Annie put her arm round Tania's shoulders and gave her a comforting hug. 'There wouldn't have been room for you and Max too,' she said, her voice gentle.

'It's OK,' said Tania. 'And we've work to do.'

Annie pushed her glasses up her nose and grinned. 'That's my girl.'

Tania smiled, surprised at Annie's flash of understanding. She looked round for Max and saw him with Andrew and Aussie. With a quick command from Andrew the dog slunk into the porch and lay down.

'He's learning,' said Max proudly.

'Aye, lad, but not the right way for us. He hasn't got it in him to work the sheep. He's only fit to be sold on.'

Her brother's face fell. 'We haven't got any sheep so it wouldn't matter to us. If I had enough money I'd buy him.'

Tania turned to Annie. 'Fancy helping me sort out the cottage?' she said.

'Leave the stove be,' said Andrew. 'The lad and I'll see to that later. We've a job to do down in the barn.'

'With the ewes?' said Max eagerly.

'If you're on for it.'

There was no doubt that Max was and Tania smiled as she and Annie walked to the cottage.

Neil could put his foot to the ground now although Tania could see it still pained him. But she had been at Slough Fell long enough to take his measure.

Smiles and encouragement were all he needed to keep him happy for the moment until the enforced idleness began to get to him. Fortunately Bill took some time in the afternoon to spread out a sheaf of plans on the kitchen table and invite his elder son to look at them with him while Tania and Annie were keeping Netta company in the sitting room.

By the time it was necessary to check the casserole she had put in the oven, the kitchen table was clear with everything rolled up and out of sight. Neil, however seemed ill at ease and she looked as him anxiously as she got the cutlery out of the drawer and laid the table.

'All this will cost a fair bit,' he said.

'And that's worrying you?'

'Aye, a bit.'

'Your father's a cautious man who'll give it a lot of thought,' she said. 'How about the two holiday cottages? Do many people come and stay in them?'

'A fair few.'

'Do you get many repeat bookings?'

'They bring their friends.'

'That's good, isn't it?'

Neil nodded, running his fingers along a crack in the wood in the table as Tania told him something of what she knew of Jake's ideas for being able to accommodate larger groups throughout the year that would be financially beneficial for the Thwaite family.

From Bill's demeanour it had seemed to her that he fully agreed and was willing to invest the money.

Neil looked up, his slow smile so like his father's lightening his face.

She thought of this during the next two days and was glad she had tried to help him. Maybe Bill had presented the information to his son as a definite

267

thing and Neil had felt side-lined. She could well understand his anxiety.

There was plenty for Annie and herself to do with cleaning the house and the cottage. They made sure the log baskets in both places were stocked with wood from the outside pile and the washing machine on full alert and the ironing done.

Annie drove down to Gillerthwaite and returned with some essentials and reported that no-one was occupying Miss Crabbe's spare room now.

Although Tania had assumed that Ivan had left, it was good to be sure. She threw herself into the polishing of the brass handles on the dresser so there wasn't time to think any more about Ivan.

By Saturday they had done all they could.

Netta had tears in her eyes when it was time for them to leave and even Bill swallowed hard once or twice.

Max was kneeling on the cold cobbles of the yard with his arms round

Aussie and his face buried in the dog's neck.

Bill and Tania exchanged glances. There was an imperceptible nod from the farmer and she smiled, grateful for his generosity to a young grieving lad who had found new solace in a life that until now seemed a sorry place.

'You'll have to ask Annie if there's room for Aussie in that small car for an excitable dog, lad,' Bill said.

Max sprang up. 'Can I? Oh, *can I*?' he cried, his face alight. 'Can we really take him home with us, Tania?'

Annie laughed. 'Don't mind me. I'm only the taxi driver.'

'Let's just see then,' Tania said. With an exaggerated gesture she threw open the car door and peered inside. 'Well, why not?'

She smiled at Max's shriek of joy. Her brother's delight in having the dog for his own helped fill an aching great hole at this moment of leave taking. She quenched the fleeting thought that Dad should be consulted first, but it vanished in the certainty that he would be happy at his son's pleasure.

Annie piled their luggage in, some of it on the back seat because there wasn't room elsewhere, but Max wasn't going to let that deter him. Aussie wasn't either. Without a backward glance he was in the car.

Bill smiled. 'So now we know how badly Aussie thinks of us.'

Max wound down the window. 'He really doesn't,' he said, giving his dog a hug. 'He's saying thank you for letting him come to live with us, aren't you Aussie?' For answer he had his face licked.

'And I'm saying thank you for what the lot of you have done for us, especially your sister.' said Bill.

Tania felt herself flush, a little tearful too. As they drove off she thought of her young brother whose confidence had grown so much over these last few days. Max was a different boy now and Jake had done that for him as well as the Thwaite family.

She didn't look back as they turned right at the top of the track and drove down the hill. Soon the farm would be out of sight, but never out of mind.

She would always remember that Slough Fell had brought her some of her happiest moments in her life. She had gained so much from being here, and she was grateful. She hoped that all of them had, even Jake.

'Fancy stopping at Miss Crabbe's shop?' Annie said as they approached Gillerthwaite. 'She said she'd be glad to see you if you had time.'

Tania brightened. 'I've plenty of time for Miss Crabbe.'

'Can I take Aussie in to show her?' asked Max.

'With a box full of kittens there?' said Tania. 'I don't think so, Max. He'd devour them instantly.'

'Aussie wouldn't hurt them, would you Aussie?' Max said, aggrieved.

They turned a bend and reached the cluster of stone buildings and Tania saw again Gillerthwaite's village shop.

So much had happened since she was here that she was almost surprised that the bell jangled in just the same way and the dim interior still smelt of beeswax and paraffin.

Smiling a welcome, Miss Crabbe stood leaning on the counter just as she had when she had come rushing to return the ginger and white kitten some days ago. But this time she struggled out from behind and enveloped Tania in a hug. Then she turned to Annie. 'And this is your friend? She was telling me about you all up at Slough Fell.'

Tania smiled, instantly at home. She bought some bread and homemade fruit cake and as Miss Crabbe was wrapping them remarked on the snow that had held them prisoner at Slough Fell. 'It's a beautiful part of the world,' she said.

Miss Crabbe's rosy cheeks dimpled as she agreed. 'And where's that young lad you brought in with you on your way through?'

'My brother, Max? He's outside in the car. Bill Thwaite has given him one of his dogs and he doesn't want to leave him there alone.'

'Aye, a responsible lad.' She reached for a jar of boiled sweets on the shelf behind her. 'Tell him next time he's to come in and see me.'

Tania smiled. 'I'll tell him.'

'For the little lad,' Miss Crabbe said as she put some sweets in a bag and handed them over with Tania's purchases. 'And how's the bigger lad who loved my kitten?'

Tania paused. 'Ah yes, Gregor. He's home now. He's OK. Really all right. You won't recognise him when you see him next, Miss Crabbe.'

'A kitten or two will be wanting a home in a few weeks. Mr Anderson'll likely be needing one.'

The door bell jangled.

'You're right there, Miss Crabbe,' a familiar voice said.

★ ★ ★

Face aflame, Tania spun round, almost dropping her purchases in her surprise at seeing Jake standing there against the light smiling at them all. He seemed to have brought a warmth in with him that immediately lifted her spirits.

'Trust you to turn up like a bad penny,' said Annie.

Jake ignored her. 'I saw the car outside with Max in it.'

'No crime in that, surely?' Annie demanded. 'And he didn't steal the dog if that's what you're thinking.'

'Be quiet, Annie.'

Tania could only stare. She had thought that Jake had gone out of her life forever and now here he was and she could think of nothing to say to him.

'We'll say farewell for the moment then, Miss Crabbe,' said Jake. 'I hope it won't be long before we see you again.'

She beamed at him. 'You'll always be right welcome, lad.'

Somehow Tania got herself outside with the others and saw that the clouds had cleared now, leaving a sky washed in pale blue. Jake's Land Rover was parked behind Annie's car, but it seemed that Max was too engrossed with Aussie to notice.

'I don't think your brother will mind if you come back in the Land Rover with me will he, Tania?' Jake said.

'But I will,' said Annie in indignation. 'Whose bright idea was it that we should stay behind so I could drive her home in the first place?'

He looked her, inscrutably. 'My plans are not that simple.'

'Obviously not.'

'I really need to talk to Tania in private, Annie, and this seemed the best way to go about it. There hasn't been much opportunity lately.'

She looked at him with her head held to one side as if considering a deep problem. 'Well no, I give you that,' she said. 'All right then. I give in. But I wouldn't if you weren't my favourite cousin, Jake, maddening as you are.'

'Don't I get any say in this?' Tania said.

Neither of them answered. Then Annie looked at her over the top of her glasses, winked and sidled towards her vehicle. 'I'll stay with Max at your house until you come home, Tania,' she promised.

'You don't need to worry about Max,' said Jake as they watched her drive off.

'Well, no. I wasn't.'

He quirked an eyebrow at her. 'You might well have been.'

'I know Max can cope. Even if he couldn't, Aussie will see he comes to no harm.'

She bathed in the warmth of his smile. 'This is high-handed of me,' he said. 'But I could think of no other way of getting you alone. I thought we'd leave the Land Rover here for a bit and walk.'

She smiled. 'Fine.' She wished she could express the happiness in her heart. Could one strangled word convey what she wanted to say?

It seemed it could because his eyes

shone. 'Come on then.'

They climbed over a stile and walked along the uphill track that had brought them here on the second day of their walk. Soon they were looking down on the village of Gillerthwaite where Miss Crabbe's shop nestled among the other stone buildings.

In the distance a curlew's evocative call disturbed the silence. Tania smelt the damp earth and felt the peaty breeze on her face. She gazed across to the far hills they hadn't been able to reach because of the snow. Traces of it still lingered up here, dotting the hillside in patches of sunlit white.

'It's beautiful,' she said.

Jake nodded. 'Bill wants us to come back here with the group and complete the walk. All of us.'

'Aussie too?' said Tania. 'I don't think Max will want to come if he had to leave his precious dog behind.'

Jake looked at her closely. 'Max is old enough to make his own decision about that, don't you think, Tania?'

'Of course he is,' she said, aware of sudden tension between them.

He smiled. 'Sorry. I shouldn't have said that. Of course you'll let him decide.'

'How can you doubt it any more?' She shot him a look filled with mischief.

'I thought the first bank holiday in May and do it over the weekend. Lambing will be finished and the baby born.'

'Baby Gregorina?' she said.

He laughed. 'The going should be a lot easier by then, especially as they know what to expect now. Collette nearly leapt out of the Land Rover when I told her we'd have another go and even Wayne was pleased. He's come on a lot, that lad, and Max had something to do with it. You too, Tania.

'He'll bring his bird book for sure,' she said.

He nodded. 'We'll be able to linger a bit more, do some bird watching. That'll please Wayne.'

'Why not put him in charge of catering? He's been an ace hand helping me with the meals, a real little worker.'

'You understand them all so well, Tania. You're a remarkable girl and I love you for it.'

She gazed at his loving, strong face, unable to speak for the joy in her heart. Then he took her chin in his hands, tilted back her head and kissed her.

'I've wanted to do that for so long,' he murmured.

'Me too,' she whispered.

'My dearest Tania, can you forgive me for being hard on you, not understanding at first your belief that being here for Netta when she needed us was of paramount importance?'

'I wasn't there for my mother,' she said, her voice low. 'No-one was because it was unexpected. But I wish I had been.'

'You think the outcome would have been different?'

She shook her head. 'I know it

279

wouldn't, but I felt guilty.'

'My poor girl. There are some things we don't understand,' he said, his voice husky. 'Just accept it, Tania, and be thankful for the time you had together.'

She took a step towards him and his mouth captured hers again. He released her for an instant, but only long enough for them to draw breath before he kissed her again.

'Would you like to share a home with me in this area, Tania?' he said at last, his voice deep with longing.

'Yes, oh yes,' she said and then was in his arms again.

'You know my dreams of converting some disused buildings and making them into a place where people, young ones, come for adventure holidays. But I also dream of making our home here too one day, yours and mine. I love this area of the Dales so much and I think you do too.'

'I'll never want to leave it.'

'We'll get to know each other properly,' he said. 'And each other's families too. Not to mention friends.'

'And Annie?'

He smiled. 'Annie's a special case. And she's been on *your* case for a while, my love, singing your praises. It was almost enough to put me off for life. I had the feeling she tripped poor Louise up on purpose so you could take her place.'

Tania's eyes danced. She wouldn't have put it past Annie either.

★　★　★

They began to walk hand in hand further on to where they could look down at the church on the outskirts of the village.

'I'd like to take a closer look at that,' he said.

Their path lead down to the road again. Jake creaked open the lynch gate to the churchyard and they went inside.

The ancient slab path ahead was gloomy and the bare branches of the stunted trees on either side loomed over them.

The door was locked, but it didn't matter. They turned away and walked across the grass to the surrounding stone wall.

Jake turned to her and looked at her closely. 'One day soon we'll be back here again when our friends and family are here to help us celebrate. A crazy idea or what?'

Tania looked at the bare trees and ancient grave stones and it seemed beautiful to her in this dazzling moment. 'Crazy and beautiful and mad and full of wonder all at the same time,' she said. 'And I don't know how that is.'

'A mystery, isn't it?'

'But not really hard to solve. I wish we had more time.'

'We will have,' he promised. 'Years and years of time. We'll have a special sort of holiday for just the two of us.'

'Another fell walk?'

'A honeymoon sort of holiday in the Dales, do you think? Or would you prefer somewhere more exotic?'

'As if I would.' She waved her hand at the surrounding fells. 'What could be more exotic than this? As long as I'm with someone I love, of course.'

His eyes twinkled. 'Of course,' he said, his voice solemn. 'As long as that someone is me.'

'Oh, I think so.'

'Then that's all right.'

Jake's laugh was deep and throaty, the dearest sound in the world. He pulled her towards him again for a brief kiss before they went out into the lane again.

THE END

We do hope that you have enjoyed reading this large print book.

Did you know that all of our titles are available for purchase?

We publish a wide range of high quality large print books including:
Romances, Mysteries, Classics
General Fiction
Non Fiction and Westerns

Special interest titles available in large print are:
The Little Oxford Dictionary
Music Book, Song Book
Hymn Book, Service Book

Also available from us courtesy of Oxford University Press:
Young Readers' Dictionary
(large print edition)
Young Readers' Thesaurus
(large print edition)

For further information or a free brochure, please contact us at:
Ulverscroft Large Print Books Ltd.,
The Green, Bradgate Road, Anstey,
Leicester, LE7 7FU, England.
Tel: (00 44) **0116 236 4325**
Fax: (00 44) **0116 234 0205**

Other titles in the
Linford Romance Library:

IN DESTINY'S WAKE

June Davies

Accused of stealing a necklace of pearls, Maud Pemberton flees Yorkshire to escape imprisonment. Henry Broome, her sweetheart, helps her begin a new life alone on the Lancashire coast. There, she encounters enigmatic innkeeper, Lawrence Kearsley, who conceals a family secret and when Henry unexpectedly arrives, Maud finds that he, too, harbours a dangerous secret ... Caught within a spiral of lies and intrigue, Maud risks all to save her love from the dreadful consequences of long-buried deception.

PROMISES OF SPRING

Jean M. Long

Sophie, who's in between jobs and recovering from a broken relationship, offers to help out her Aunt Rose in Kent. Reluctantly, she finds herself being drawn into village affairs. Keir Ellison, a neighbour, is heavily involved in plans for a Craft Centre, but there is much opposition from the older residents who have different ideas for the old chapel. Sophie is attracted to Keir, but soon realises he's a man of mystery. Can she trust him?

LOVE IN PERIL

Phyllis Mallett

1792: Travelling on the long journey from London to Cornwall to meet her estranged father, Hester is plunged into peril when her coach is held up. She escapes and narrowly avoids falling victim to smugglers, due to the timely appearance of Hal Trevian. Hal takes her to her father, but, instead of finding security, other problems arise . . . although Hal is always there to support her. Will their interest in each other ever turn to love?

FAMILY HOLIDAY

Denise Robins

The summer for Clare, Guy and the children brought the holiday — like every other year. It also brought the chance meeting with Blake Randall, the young officer she'd loved years ago in a wartime hospital. And whereas Guy was the kindly but unexciting doctor she had married, Blake and Clare felt the same spark of their youth. Soon they were unashamedly head over heels in love again, but when the holiday ended, she would be separated from Blake forever . . .

SOME EIGHTEEN SUMMERS

Lillie Holland

After eighteen years living a sheltered life as a vicar's daughter in Norfolk, Debbie Meredith takes work as a companion to the wealthy Mrs Caroline Dewbrey in Yorkshire. Travelling by train, she meets the handsome and charming Hugh Stacey. However, before long, Debbie is wondering why Mrs Dewbrey lavishes so much attention on her. And what of her son Alec's stance against her involvement with Hugh? Debbie then finds that she's just a pawn embroiled in a tragic vendetta . . .

THE GIRL FROM YESTERDAY

Teresa Ashby

Robert Ashton and Kate Gibson are a month away from their wedding. However, Robert's ex-wife Caroline turns up from Australia with a teenage daughter, Karen, who Robert knew nothing about. Then, as Caroline and Robert spend time together, they still seem to have feelings for one another, despite the fact that Jim, back in Australia, has asked Caroline to marry him. Now, Robert and Caroline must decide whether their futures lie with each other — or with Kate and Jim.

SPECIAL MESSAGE TO READERS

THE ULVERSCROFT FOUNDATION
(registered UK charity number 264873)
was established in 1972 to provide funds for research, diagnosis and treatment of eye diseases. Examples of major projects funded by the Ulverscroft Foundation are:-

- The Children's Eye Unit at Moorfields Eye Hospital, London
- The Ulverscroft Children's Eye Unit at Great Ormond Street Hospital for Sick Children
- Funding research into eye diseases and treatment at the Department of Ophthalmology, University of Leicester
- The Ulverscroft Vision Research Group, Institute of Child Health
- Twin operating theatres at the Western Ophthalmic Hospital, London
- The Chair of Ophthalmology at the Royal Australian College of Ophthalmologists

You can help further the work of the Foundation by making a donation or leaving a legacy. Every contribution is gratefully received. If you would like to help support the Foundation or require further information, please contact:

THE ULVERSCROFT FOUNDATION
The Green, Bradgate Road, Anstey
Leicester LE7 7FU, England
Tel: (0116) 236 4325

website: www.foundation.ulverscroft.com